RETURN TO TEXAS

Al Boyd

iUniverse, Inc.
New York Lincoln Shanghai

RETURN TO TEXAS

iUniverse, Inc.

For information address:
iUniverse, Inc.
2021 Pine Lake Road, Suite 100
Lincoln, NE 68512
www.iuniverse.com

ISBN: 0-595-31536-4

Printed in the United States of America

Dedicated to Gail Roy who helped and encouraged me to write this story.

CHAPTER 1

▼

The warm westerly wind blew sideways at the rider as he hunched down under his hat, his shoulders drawn down tight as he leaned at an angle into the wind. He was a solitary figure on a dark colored roan riding deliberately northward down the dusty, rutted wagon road. Slowly the familiar landscape began to relax him, and the wind sensing its home to be close at hand, also began to ease.

Jed Garrett, the eldest son of Tom and Edith Garrett, was coming home. How soothingly the word home rang in his mind as he repeated it over again in his head. But what would he be returning to? Would he even fit in?

Ahead, through the dust and haze, the outline of the Black Pine Mountains faintly appeared. The familiar sights of past years now rushed to his mind. How long had it been since he left to fight in the bitter war with Mexico and Santa Anna. His mind counted back. He was twenty, almost twenty-one, when he enlisted in the army. Now, two years, later he was returning home. He looked and felt like he had been gone much longer.

It had been by the stroke of a pen and the whim of an army lieutenant that Jed was assigned to the Texas Rangers as a wrangler when he enlisted. Most new enlistees were issued a single shot musket, but the Rangers were using the new Colt repeating revolvers. Technically it was known as a "Colt Number Five Texas Paterson". The Paterson had already proved itself to the Rangers prior to the war when fifteen men under the leadership of John Hays attacked a band of eighty Comanche Indians with spectacular results by killing or wounding over one half of the war party. As a result almost every Ranger wore the long barreled sidearm.

Later, when Jed signed up with the army and ultimately ended up in the Rangers, Ben McCulloch bent the rules when they issued the repeater to him, saying he wanted his unit well armed, "and that meant everyone!" The Paterson was large for a hand held weapon with a barrel nearly twelve inches long and the trigger dropped down only when the hammer was cocked back, but it had served well. More than once he owed his life to the rapid firing Colt.

Only five short months ago the army issued a new "Colt Walker" to the Rangers and it was a vast improvement over the older Paterson model. It was lighter having a barrel length of approximately seven inches long, a newly designed fixed trigger protected by a trigger guard and held five rounds in a revolving cylinder. And once again this newer model repeating Colt quickly became the favored weapon of choice.

In March 1848 the men heard that the Treaty of Guadalupe Hidalgo was signed in Mexico City in early February ending the Mexican-American War. Within days men were being mustered out but Jed had to remain with his unit for another month as he was responsible for the final disposition of the livestock.

The majority of the horses were sold at auction and bought by the owners of outlying ranches whose ranch hands were often Mexicans and intermingled with a few Negro hands. The rest of the horses were usually bought by the owners of the large lucrative cotton plantations in east Texas. Cotton was still king in southeastern Texas and a cheap labor force was deemed a necessity by the growers. Most of the black men around were owned as slaves although a few had brought their freedom and had hired out as free men around the area. Thus a variety of all colors and nationalities of man rounded out the population in Harrisburg which was close to the gulf port city of Galveston. It was into this mix of humanity that the army continued the processing of men back into civilian life.

As the men were mustered out they were given a chance to buy their new Walker Colts for the sum of eight dollars. Almost all the men who used the repeaters during the war chose the option to purchase the government revolvers for themselves, Jed included.

But those were days past and his future lay ahead. He was now relaxed and basked in serenity as he rode northward down the rutted and worn wagon path in the open prairie. In the distance an old adobe building lay crumbling in the harsh extremes of the severe summer and winter climate. All that now remained were three of its adobe walls. The roof and front wall had long since fallen in. Remains of the adjoining horse corral had fallen as well, the rubble bearing a silent testimony of an earlier attempt to subdue the wild land and to eke out a living for a poor family. Only four crooked juniper fence posts prevailed as sentinels standing in this wasteland of cactus and sagebrush. A dirty red piece of bandana was fluttering in the wind on one of the remaining posts.

Jed rode up slowly, allowing his horse to conserve energy for the long trip ahead. The rag piqued his curiosity and nearing the post, he bent down to his left over the saddle to retrieve it.

The impact knocked him sideways as his frightened horse bolted and Jed toppled out of the saddle. He saw a piece of cactus with a cluster of sharp needles and some old horse tracks in the dirt and then heard the echo of the rifle shot. The fall to the ground took an eternity. Time stood still as he spied larger chunks of adobe and small red rock fragments beside the post during his plunge to the ground. He knew from past experience he had been shot and he tried to reach out and brace himself for the impact but his arms would not move. He dropped like a heavy stone and struck the ground head first. On his face and left shoulder he lay with his hips twisted grotesquely in the opposite direction. The blood was running from his head, right arm and shoulder. The world became black as the daylight disappeared.

*   *   *   *

With rifles drawn menacingly, three riders approached from the easterly slope, pushing their mounts hard as they rode down off the bench. Dust flew from around the horses' hooves as they were reigned to an abrupt stop.

"My God, that's not the old man! It's a young guy!" gasped one of the riders.

"Damn it, I told you to wait until we got closer," screamed another.

"Who is it?"

"Hell, I don't know," replied the first.

Sizing up the situation one of the riders cried, "It makes no difference now. We've got to get out of here and make sure we aren't seen. Quick, grab his horse. He's dead anyway and he sure as hell don't need it now. Leave everything else!" He continued, "Come on. Let's get the hell outta' here!"

The third rider quickly and obediently spurred his mount and soon had the roan in tow. Hurriedly the men turned their horses northward riding frantically up the dusty and ancient trail, their tracks soon blending in among the spore left by earlier travelers.

*   *   *   *

Evening comes with a rush to the desert. The afternoon breeze stopped as if on signal and darkness had set in for the night and with the darkness came the early desert chill of fall. The clear evening sky slowly surrendered to the awakening stars.

The crumpled figure by the warped posts started to moan softly. Slowly the nighttime chill was starting to restore consciousness to Jed. As he lay, groans of pain passed through his lips. Sluggishly he tried to open his eyes. He could see nothing from his right eye and felt the dirt from the ground on the other side of his face. He gingerly raised his head; the pain was wrenching! By squinting he could focus with his left eye, but was forced by the pain to drop his face back down again in the dust and the dirt. At last his brain began to function and he knew he must roll over on his back. His head reeled with waves of pain as he tried to move his left arm out from under his body.

"Take your time," he told himself.

As he lay on his left shoulder, next to a post near the back of his neck, another wave of pain passed through his head and torso making him groan in pain. He forced himself to concentrate. "I have to get on my back."

He lay in the dirt gathering his strength as he knew what pain might follow such a maneuver. Slowly, he forced his left arm out from under his chest and set his palm face down in the dirt while straightening his legs. Poised, he waited, gathering both strength and the will to push himself over. The throes of pain were becoming unbearable. Patiently and resolutely, he waited, took a gasping breath and gave a hard push. He was shocked to hear someone scream. Then he realized it was he.

The stars began to shine brilliantly while the evening chill of the desert continued to set in, the night creatures wakening to continue their pursuit of life. Gnats, insects, moths, field mice and coyotes began scurrying about seeking their evening meal by hunting each other and quenching their thirst from the nighttime dew. A pair of night owls flew almost silently as their keen eyesight searched for prey. The dark sky reflected on a occasional bat swooping down for a meal of the nocturnal flying creatures. The vast desert plains were now alive and spewing forth life that only hours before lay hidden in this seemingly desolate and sterile land.

Two hours of chill were enough to rouse Jed back to awareness for a second time. Lying on his back, slowly regaining his senses, he could see the dominance of the milky way.

His mind raced with questions. "Was the bushwhacker a robber? Was his horse still around or did someone take the horse? Was his saddle or even his money reason enough that he would kill for it? Was it someone he knew? Was he still out there in the darkness waiting?" Now his survival instincts, though jumbled, pushed to seek protection from his attacker.

Sadly he recalled he paid twelve dollars of his mustering out pay to buy the roan from Richard King who had also just been released from the army. King wanted to start up ranching in the area and invested his money quickly in a small remuda comprised of some fifty horses. As they wished each other well and parted company, King told him he just received a small contract to supply horses and cattle to some ranches just west of San Antonio. No one knew of the impact King would later have in the growth of the Texas Territory.

Jed realized too, his fine Mexican engraved leather saddle and saddlebags were gone along with the horse. The saddle alone had set him back thirty dollars, not to mention the loss of a rifle, his bedroll, water, some spiced jerky and the rest of his mustering out pay. All five hundred and thirty dollars gone!

One of the worst crimes, next to murder in this new west, was horse thievery. A man without a horse in a country as large as the Texas Territory was usually a man condemned to a slow agonizing death from the sun. The thieves that were caught died rapidly, usually at the end of a rope. This was so entrenched in the minds of the Texans that it usually stopped anyone from even staying near a suspected thief, as guilt by association can also be deadly.

Suddenly remembering, he felt for his Colt. The Walker was still in its holster. Relieved, he thought to himself, I've got to clean it of any dirt that might have stopped up the barrel. Another major question tumbled forth, "Why hadn't his attacker taken the gun?" Thinking back, he realized that it was probably hidden by his body, or at least partially concealed from view. Perhaps too, the bushwhacker's need for the horse was greater than his need for another firearm. Nothing made any sense now, just questions and no answers came to mind.

Still extremely weak, he managed to drag himself up to a sitting position. Then by pulling on the post with his left arm, he weakly stood up, paused and listened. Nothing. Not a sound. "Is he still out there?" Another unanswered question. "Could it have been a Comanche? Not likely," he decided, "as I've still got my hair."

"Damn," he said aloud. Whoever it was could come back he realized as he looked desperately for something to provide some protection.

In the bright moonlight he could see the dark looming shape of the run-down adobe hut. The remains of the hovel would have to hide him from his new foe, or foes, and he moved towards the structure. Due to the loss of blood he felt lightheaded which caused his legs to teeter precariously and each step required a profound effort. He moved slowly and painstakingly across the twelve foot distance to one of the standing side walls, pausing there to gather his strength. Carefully brushing his boot quietly back and forth amid the rubble on the dirt floor he began inching himself towards the back wall. The boot maneuver was a safety precaution tending to send the scorpions, tarantulas and black widow spiders scurrying when one is moving into a dark, unknown space. This he had learned from his association with the Rangers. At last, he carefully and slowly eased himself down against the old adobe wall.

Seated with his back in a corner, Jed reached for his Colt Walker with his left hand, blowing out any of the debris that may have jammed in the barrel. "It will have to do for now—I'll clean it later," he mumbled. Temporarily satisfied with this cursory inspection he laid the weapon in readiness across his lap. Methodically he began to assess his own condition. The bullet hit the back of his upper right arm, creased the top of the same shoulder and the back of his head. Undoubtedly the shot happened just as he reached down for the cloth rag on the fence post. Lucky for me, he reasoned, if one could figure this to be lucky.

As he leaned his head gingerly back against the cool adobe, he tried again to make some sense of what happened, but his recent exertion made his mind hazy and concentration difficult. Wearily, he pushed the questions away and just sat listening. His senses trying to regroup as he awaited his invisible foe. The only noises he heard were the normal sounds of the desert creatures themselves at night. These night sounds reassured him, as he knew if there were total quiet, his adversary may be moving around. This noisy quietness represented a friendly respite, so at last Jed could sleep, a strength regaining sleep.

Gradually the morning sun, slyly brazen, shone over the top of the east adobe wall. Slowly it began its morning search of the landscape, cautiously beginning it's climb of assenting approval into the heavens. Bright shafts of sunlight now peeked over the horizon. The sun rose, pushing forth the light and warmth of a new day on the returning wounded man.

Jed opened his eyes. The heat from the morning sun felt almost luxurious on his sore body, this same sun which could be devastating during the day to the unprotected. He carefully took new measure of himself. Brushing off dirt and matted blood from the back of his head, he felt where the bullet had creased his scalp. A tangle of blood and hair came from his head. Unseeing, but carefully, he used his hand to brush as much dirt as possible from the wound. Carefully too, he also wiped his face and eyes of blood and grit.

Undoing the neckerchief around his neck, and using his good left arm and his teeth, he tore it into four long pieces. These he tied together in a line to make a sling for his right arm, knowing that the tighter he could tie the arm down the less it would hurt with any movement. "This will have to do for now," he said aloud as he put his head through the loop. Groaning, he slowly rose while leaning against the adobe wall for support.

"Hell, how could I have been so damn stupid as to let down my guard and get ambushed like that?" he asked himself. His prior army experiences honed his survival senses and his instinct had saved his life before, but this time he let down his guard.

"Damn!" he cursed himself again for mentally falling asleep. He knew he had relaxed while daydreaming about returning to the safety and security of home.

"A good way to get killed. Well, it won't happen again." Still, he had been lucky and he knew it.

How far was home? Reasoning, it was a least a seven to ten day walk to the Brazos River, then hopefully he might be able to meet up with a fellow traveler and borrow a horse for the ride into the town of Wedgewood. The tiny town was wedged in between the foothills west of the Black Pine Mountains, hence its name. There, Doc Winters could clean and bandage his wounds before he would continue the ride to the "Lazy G" ranch.

Right now the situation was acute. His canteen had been tied to his saddle so now he faced this long trek in this scorching heat without water. Furthermore, remaining vigilant against another possible attack, and knowing another lapse could prove lethal, would be a real undertaking. He knew any possibility of help riding by on this ancient north-south trail was extremely remote.

The choice was easy to make. If he stayed, he could die out here before anyone might come by. If he reached the Brazos river road it was possible to survive.

Resolutely he stepped out from the adobe shack's broken walls into the brilliant morning sun. Near the post where he had fallen lay his hat. Gratefully, he made his way over, and bending his knees gingerly, retrieved the hat. After knocking off the caked dirt and blood against one of the remaining posts, he attempted to straighten it to its former shape without much success. Then, mindful of the wound in his scalp, he carefully placed it on his head. Although his head still hurt, it was familiar and comforting to put the hat on. He realized the hat should help prevent heat dehydration along the way to the river, if he got to the river!

Alongside the juniper posts were the horseshoe tracks of two, possibly three riders. One of the set of prints could have been made by his own horse and he looked out over the landscape hoping to see the roan, but it was not to be.

Turning and peering to the north, he could make out the dim, low edges of the Black Pine Mountains. The river came down from the northern territories through the mountains and turned east after it passed near the hamlet of Wedge-wood, then south again on its trip to the Gulf of Mexico.

With a watchful glance at the surrounding range, the walk began. The sun was halfway up in the morning sky and for now the temperature would be bearable. His plan would be to travel in the cool of the mornings and to rest under an Indian style sagebrush canopy during the peak temperatures of the day's heat. He could travel again in the evenings, and if the night skies were clear he would push on at night, using the Big Dipper and the North Star to guide his way.

He set out with his eyes focused on the faint mountain outline. From this angle the mountains looked to be cool and inviting, but he knew from experience that there was not much shade, or anything else, to be found on those hills. Even the deer found the foraging meager. There were a few scraggly pinon pines near the summits. He knew too, that the Indians picked the pinon nuts for their winter larder there, and he had picked them too as a young boy. But the main thing was to keep going towards the base of the hills. There he would eventually find the road that came west from Austin, the new capitol of Texas, as it meandered in a northerly fashion along the Brazos river. Most importantly there would be water.

The sun rose higher in the sky and he squinted as he looked into the distance, his face hardened and set by many past long rides into the tempestuous elements of nature. The knots from his makeshift sling dug into his neck as he unconsciously pulled on the sling to reposition them. Soon a slight breeze came up from the north, and although welcome, he knew it was only a temporary reprieve.

As Jed walked he thought back to the war he had been involved in. It had been a brutal clash of titans brought on by the ever westward movement of the Americans. Settlers, ranchers, farmers and opportunists from every class of society came in ever larger numbers to Texas. The hordes of new Americans took over the lands by purchase, squatting and even by thievery. These lands were rightly owned by Mexico, but any Mexican attempt to govern and collect taxes for its government was met with angry and intense resistance.

Texas eventually established the Texas Rangers to protect their newly acquired interests. Many of these men were extremely ruthless and they exacted a fear among the Mexican peoples as they enforced their own brand of law upon Texas which including running off the present owners, shootings, rape and pillaging, all under the guise of so called righteousness.

The Mexican government felt the aggressive Americans wanted to take all of it's territory which included Texas, New Mexico, Arizona, Nevada, Utah and all of the California territory as well. Quite naturally they mobilized to protect their holdings and their people already living on these lands. It did not matter that they were spread too thin to govern the area in question. At the same time the Americans felt that all the lands clear to the Pacific Ocean were theirs for the taking. The Americans called it their 'Manifest Destiny' to own all this land. The clash of arms was inevitable.

In early 1846 General Zachary Taylor began to amass troops at Corpus Christi, Texas as a show of strength to Mexico. The massacre at the Alamo in 1836, some ten years earlier, became the central focus of the time and so there was no lack of recruits. The American armies consisted of the regulars and thousands of volunteers who rushed to enlist bringing the total man power to nearly seventy thousand men.

Most of the volunteers were normally issued single shot, rod and primer muskets, fired by a spark from the flints. These firearms were often unreliable when the flint and powder got wet or damp. Muskets of similar type were used throughout the Mexican armies. However, some of the regiments in the American regulars were issued the new percussion rifles, most of which were made by Colt's Patent Arms Manufacturing Company of New Jersey. The percussion weapons had a watertight cap which held powder and was ignited by a hammer blow rather than by the spark method. It was a big improvement and in many of the battles that ensued where the Americans were severely outnumbered, quite often the difference in the outcome of these skirmishes was due to the superiority of these new weapons.

At the beginning of the conflict the Texas Rangers were put under the command of Colonel John Hays in the army. Hays was also known to the men under him as Jack Hays. Since the Rangers' knowledge of the area was impressive, it was only natural that they were to act as scouts for the army. The Rangers were then divided into two groups under Hays, one led by Sam Walker and other led by Ben McCulloch. It was said around the campfires that because of input from Sam Walker to Samuel Colt, the Colt Walker was named for Sam Walker.

Jed had served and fought under McCulloch and General 'Zach' Taylor, from the battles at Resaca de la Palma and Palo Alto through Cammargo, Mier, Cerralvo and on to Monterrey. He participated in the terrible hand-to-hand fighting on the hills of Independencia and Federacion outside Monterrey. He had been decorated more than once, baptized by the brutality of war and its moral debauchery. Jed had learned his lessons well. His government issued rifle initially replaced by the Colt Paterson percussion repeating revolver and now more recently by the Colt Walker rested in his well worn holster. His Bowie knife too and its sheath had become comfortable, like well worn battle decorations pointing out—here was someone to reckon with.

After the fall of Monterrey to the American army, General Winfield Scott took many of the seasoned troops, including Captain Walker's detachment of Rangers for his attack on Mexico City. Jed remained with Ben McCulloch's group dealing out army style justice to the remaining guerrilla loyalists still fighting in the defense of Mexico.

Thousands on both sides died in the struggle. Many of his army friends and acquaintances became just so many bodies blown apart in the war. The sight of bleeding arms and legs, many separated from their bodies, still plagued him in the darkness of many sleepless nights. At his mustering out he heard from his army friend, Richard King, that Captain Walker had also been killed in Mexico City.

Jed often wondered why he survived? Why were the lives of his companions not spared? Why all the deaths of young men which had so much to live for? He could think of no answer other than fate. These horrible thoughts and memories he pushed and suppressed from his mind as he continued his trek northward.

The warm sun soon produced a river of sweat down the center of his back and dampened his shirt. His holstered revolver rode on his right hip with a rawhide loop drawn across the hammer of the weapon to make it secure. With an upward push from his thumb, he could quickly draw the gun although his right arm now was out of commission. He was not as fast on the draw as the men he had worked and ridden with. Rangers Smith, McCulloch, and even "Bigfoot" Wallace, told him, "It's not speed so much as accuracy that counts." And Jed was quite accurate. His accuracy came from hunting game with a single shot musket back on the "Lazy G". There always was a need to supplement the food supply when living so far from the nearest town. One shot was usually all you got as necessity taught accuracy. Later, unlike many others, he found it easy to adapt from the rifle to the hand held pistols. Now the Colt repeater was the weapon of choice and very few people owned one. Fortunately his attacker missed the opportunity to own his.

He walked with the gait of an older rider as he pitched ever so slightly from side to side with each step. His dusty boots were made of top quality leather were hand crafted by skilled Mexican labor as he had them made in Monterrey by one of the best artisans in the city. As he walked along the old dirt roadway the rowels of his spurs made an occasional noise as they turned. At the same time he continued to keep an anxious watch for any signs of human life, be it friend or foe, for he knew he would need food and water before long.

The sun continued its intense assault. The sweat from his forehead ran down into his face making his eyes sting and he could feel the dampness on his back as well. Later he knew his exposed skin would become dry, parched and burnt. Stooping down he picked up a piece of rock and put it into his mouth, knowing it would help keep his mouth moist. It helps, he had learned. Waves of heat rose down the rutted road in front of him. The sun was now almost directly overhead.

"Time to stop," he muttered softly to no one in particular.

At the side of the trail he picked out a large sage bush. Breaking off the larger branches that would come free, he tossed them over a nearby group of three smaller sage bushes to form a canopy of shade away from the hot blistering sun.

Not too bad, he thought as he squatted down underneath. It would have to do for now. His shoulder and arm were noticeably sore and he winced when trying to lie back to get comfortable. He pulled his hat down over his eyes to provide some relief and respite from the hot sun. This would not be easy he realized as he tried to relax. The heat of the day had just started and the Black Pine Mountains seemed no closer at hand.

How long had he walked? Two, three, four hours? He must have covered at least ten miles, but he knew distance in the desert is deceiving. A battalion of ants now attacked his legs and arms. Rest was not possible as he swatted them away. What makes them find a person so quickly?

With his good arm Jed swatted away another ant from his neck as time inched by slowly. Each minute seemed an hour, each hour an eternity. He forced himself to wait, knowing what the risks might be if he continued to push on through the heat of the day. Water would be so good now, he thought, then quickly he pushed the subject from his conscious mind. Back came his mind to water again, then on to food. His stomach was now asking for its respite, as he realized he had not eaten since having a bit of beef jerky and a hard roll for breakfast the day before. Continually he pushed his mind away from the two subjects at hand. The gnats, as well as the ants, were determined to give his body no peace as they pressed forth their relentless attacks.

At last the sun started its slide from high noon towards the horizon. He waited uncomfortably about an hour before darkness before he deliberately and cautiously rose from under the sagebrush canopy, then stiffly stepped out again down the old roadway. I must go 'till the late darkness of night, he said to himself. I need to travel when it's cooler. I can rest tomorrow.

As he walked in the evening dusk he thought of the Lazy G Ranch and wondered of his parents and younger brother. "Let's see, James was three years younger. That would make him eighteen now." Pleasantly he recalled the scraps the two brothers had endured, namely wrestling and name calling the way siblings do. He began to have doubts if he would even be able to recognize his towhead brother now.

His mother's pleasant smiling face appeared to his memory. She was tall at five foot nine and of Scandinavian extraction with the typical clear skin and blond hair. Her family originally came to America from England and settled in Virginia. It was a hard life but Edith had the strength required as she supported her family wherever needed. She always worked beside his father, whether it was a roundup, branding or even fending off an infrequent Indian war party passing through the family homestead.

'Pa' was the pillar of strength for the entire family to rely and draw upon. Standing six feet four inches, Tom weighed close to two hundred and forty-five pounds. His large stature coupled with a firm and steady facial expression made men recognize that here was a force to be cautious of. A man of Puritan stock committed to firm work ethics, he was often demanding upon his family. Long days of hard work were the norm for the Garrett family. Jed, being the eldest, had the family chores thrust on him from an early age and consequently James reaped the benefit of watching Jed to see how he performed. As a result Jed was the object of his father's impatient criticism. As James became old enough to do some of the chores, he was shown more favoritism as he had learned from his older brother's failures.

His father's same intense drive was also concentrated in Jed. The determination of the two strong minds clashed repeatedly as Jed grew into his teen years.

The prolonged Mexican saber rattling had been the cause for the Texas Territory to raise an army and each family was asked to send a man to serve and protect. Thousands of new Texas Americans rushed at the call to enlist, and Jed used the army draft as an excuse to get out from under his father's rigid domination. It was painful to leave his family that day two years ago, but Jed felt he must escape; the ambition and restlessness of youth made the move imperative. He was sure his father knew and felt the same frustration but the two were unable to cross the barriers of stubbornness that were being raised between them. How would his father now accept Jed's return? That was the unknown.

He stumbled and came back to the present. His head began to throb with each step and every jolt continually jarred his arm and shoulder in the makeshift sling. The pain persisted. He planned to walk until late in the evening to take advantage of the coolness of the night air. Now his head hurt so badly he realized that he would not be able to go as far as he had originally intended.

The early moonlight shone brightly as Jed peered out under the brim of his hat searching for a partially protected spot from any piercing eyes. He saw a slight indentation on one of the low ridges ahead. He walked towards one of the mounds and staggered off the road pathway. Too tired to care, he dropped to the ground, sitting, then lying back flat on his back.

His head pounded from the pain of day's exertion. Trying to rest, he closed his eyes to the stars above; his arm still continued to throb as he tried to relax and sleep. After nearly an hour he finally dozed off. His body had to have rest, water and food. The water and food would have to wait.

A rustle in the bushes woke him. Jed opened his eyes to early morning daylight, his senses now on alert. He heard the noise again. "A rabbit," he thought. Slowly with his left hand he reached across his stomach and released the leather strap holding the weapon in its holster. Carefully he withdrew the gun and began to speculate on a rabbit breakfast. He moved ever so slightly and the jack rabbit shot from the brush by his feet. It was too fast, and it was gone. "Damn!" he muttered as he raised up hoping for another glimpse and another chance, but it was not to be.

He had slept reasonably well, but much later than he had intended. Now sitting up, he slowly rose to his feet. Stiffness had set in his arm and shoulder making him wince as he tested it. I'll keep the sling on, he thought as he carefully looked around to be certain he had not missed something or someone. He noted a slight swelling in his arm as he squeezed it. In six, maybe eight days, he should be at the river. There he could rest and clean his wounds as he waited for help from a passing traveler. The sun seemed warmer than usual for this early in the morning, but the thought quickly evaporated from his mind as he set off on his trek.

"Today I will not push quite as hard," he mumbled through parched and dry lips. "I've got to conserve strength for the journey ahead." A hawk soared high in the morning warm air currents searching for its breakfast. Jed knew it was out of the range of his pistol. He became resigned, "So much for my breakfast too."

His pace began to slacken as the morning sun rose high into the sky. I'll go on for another hour or so, and he mentally made a note to balance his strength against the searing heat of the bright sun. Even so, his strength was beginning to ebb as he walked on. Two, three times he stumbled, not falling, but Jed was now forcing his mind and body to function. Instinct finally made Jed seek refuge from the hot sun. A group of juniper trees lay ahead alongside the trail. Upon reaching the trees Jed collapsed on the ground under them. Sleep came almost immediately.

CHAPTER 2

▼

The slight whisper of the southwest wind carried a faint distant noise of shouting and hoof beats up the trail which suddenly woke Jed. A band of Indians was approaching from the south back down the wagon trail. He quickly pulled himself behind the trees keeping the scraggly tree bases between him and the approaching band. Drawing his Colt, he realized it was a large Comanche raiding party of at least fifteen braves with twenty to thirty extra horses in tow. Besides their lances, at least half of the party were carrying Mexican style muskets. They had evidently been on a foray into Mexico and were now returning home with their bounty.

At first it had been the Kiowa and the Apache who ruled the land. Later in the early 1700's the fierce Comanche came down from the northern plains. The Comanche were extremely brutal and eventually pushed the Kiowa as well as the Apache tribes out of the territory forcing them hundreds of miles to the west. By the early 1800's even the Comanche were being decimated and pushed out by the new white settlers, but though they were declining in numbers they still continued their raids upon other tribes, the Mexicans and the white settlers so Jed was determined to take no chances.

"This is no time to be stupid," he reasoned as he ducked down lower, knowing he was obviously out manned. Even though his firepower was superior, it still would not be much help against all of those braves. And even with his repeating Colt, he knew he couldn't escape if they circled and attacked. It was definitely a losing situation. Cautiously he watched and saw they were tracking something ahead of them! With a start, he realized, "Oh, my God! It's me!"

Quickly, yet keeping low, he backed down behind the scraggly juniper's screen of branches. Turning away he began running while bending down close towards the ground. Now with more trees between him and the war party he began to run faster and with abandon. His aching shoulder and arm were no longer a concern as he began a run for his life. Fear brought forth an adrenaline burst of energy.

Down through the bottoms of the draws he raced. He was now in front of the party by about one mile, but he knew when the Indians saw his tracks running away from the stand of junipers they would spur their ponies hard in an effort to catch up to him. He was now their quarry. As he ran he realized the predicament he was in and slowly an idea began to form.

Stopping quickly he began to backtrack, stepping in his own tracks when available, and stepping on rocks when possible. Going back about an eighth of a mile, he then left his old trail. Carefully now, he used his hand and a small branch of sage to wipe out any traces of track showing this new direction. At the same time he broke off tiny pieces of the sage, letting them fall upon the lightly brushed reddish brown soil to give the appearance of an undisturbed riparian landscape. This should gain him perhaps another half hour in which to shake his pursuers if at all possible.

Gasping for air he resumed his desperate flight. He crossed three more draws again taking the time to erase his tracks. Far in the distance he heard the exuberant cries of the braves as they picked up his trail by the edge of the rutted dirt road. Panting for breath he tried to settle into a long even stride so he could pace himself for the perilous race for his life.

Night will soon be coming and that will help, he reasoned. If he could last until darkness it would help slow their pursuit. He looked back, no sign of them yet, but he knew they were coming. A scalp from a white man would be a powerful coup among their people and too tempting to pass up, especially when the bait was on foot.

As he silently ran, he urgently besieged the sun to hasten down from the heavens, at the same time forcing his body to put as much distance as possible from the war party. Time and distance would determine his life.

He could hear the sporadic excited cries of the braves now.

"My God, they're getting closer!" He tried to force himself to react in a calm manner. "Your only chance is to keep on a steady pace. Stay rational, stay calm," he cautioned himself as if he were talking to another person.

Sagebrush, sand burrs, goatheads and cactus needles ripped savagely at his clothes, opening numerous cuts and scratches that were starting to bleed. Yet he was unaware of these cuts and scrapes as he pushed on towards the limit of his endurance. Running with a long stride he moved rapidly across the flats, slowing only as he dropped down into the arroyos. He ran for a time in the ravines, out of view, then coming up onto the bench land again he pushed on.

The sun finally dropped below the horizon as he looked back before moving down into another gully. In the distance he could make out only two riders after him. The rest of the war party obviously remained together to herd the horses and to move their triumphantly won trophies toward their main camp far north of the Brazos.

He ran on into the dusk. Clouds, he begged. Clouds. An extremely dark night might allow his escape. No cloud cover would allow his pursuers to still follow his tracks in the bright moonlight and eventually overtake him. A star began to shine in the skies ahead, then two, three, as thousands more became visible in the heavens. He began to stumble as the shadows from the low lying brush obscured his vision and he had to slow his pace to keep from tripping and falling more often.

Slowly he began to realize that the Indians would figure out that he was headed for the Brazos River. Time and the advantage was with them. Even if they lost his trail he knew they could simply continue toward the river, then lie in wait for him to approach their trap. Recognizing this, he turned directly to the east. Hopefully his pursuers would push on northwards towards the river and he would be able to stop and rest.

Continuing east for another hour he came to a small rise that completely devoured his last remaining bit of energy. He fell, then crawled under a clump of sage. His exhausted body was completely consumed by his need for rest and sleep.

After six hours the screech of a night owl nudged Jed from his deep slumber. Lying on his stomach, his face in the dirt, his bearings slowly began to return. Morning was arriving. He groaned out loud as he pushed himself up to a sitting position. "How long have I slept? Am I still being chased?"

It appeared that his diversion tactics may have bought him some time. The hunters had temporarily lost their prey.

His legs ached and as the morning light increased he realized just how bad the toll had been to his body. His fine made leather boots were being cut to shreds. His buckskin trousers were also beginning to shred from the thorns encountered during his dash for safety. Blood, dirt and dust had begun to mat together. His shoulder now ached with every movement. His every fiber cried out for water and food. He was in a very dangerous condition and he knew it. His only salvation lay in reaching the Brazos.

He rose on aching legs with trembling muscles that were reluctant to respond. With extreme effort he forced his first cautious steps northward in the direction of the river. As the sun slowly rose thirst began its relentless assault on his tired and faltering frame.

"I must get to the river," he gasped inaudibly through parched and split lips.

All movement was now automatic as his brain ceased conscious thought while the sun continued its parching rise into the sky. His body became numb to the attack of the cactus and the prickly pear. Jed took on another appearance, one of a gaunt, staggering and mobile scarecrow. No thoughts now, just forward tottering steps, his stiff legs stumbling as he moved forward in his trancelike walk. Intermittent periods of foggy conscious awareness wove in and out as he staggered forward and cursed at the sun.

He fell again face down next to a small cactus. He lay staring at the stubby plant which was about eighteen inches high. Slowly his brain and eyes focused. Eventually the thought of water in the cactus came forth. Slowly and painfully he reached down and taking out his Bowie knife he began to hack on the plant. The needles gouged into his hands as he cut a fist sized hole in the cactus. He reached in and took out a handful of pulp and pushed it into his mouth. The coarse woody interior was tasteless. He continued to lie there on the ground and chew. Finally he felt saliva and knew that he was getting some moisture from the core.

Jed lay there straining the moisture from the plant for nearly an hour. Slowly strength seeped into his tired and aching body. His torso shook as he forced himself to rise again on his sore and wobbly legs to resume his walk.

How long had it been? Three, four days? He lost count. He only knew he must reach the river. The heart of the cactus would not provide enough substance for survival, of this he was certain.

More rational again, he tried counting his steps in a muted tone. "One, two, three," and on and on........, "eighty, eighty-one, eighty-two, ninety two, ninety-three." He lost count and started again. "One, two, three,—."

"Yi, yi, yi, yi, yi!" The war whoops brought him to an abrupt stop! Two braves on horses were riding straight for him. With his left hand he drew his Colt and fired just as the nearest brave fired his musket. Both shots missed! Jed fired again and the second shot hit the Indian in his chest knocking him off of his horse. As the brave fell Jed saw the look of shock and anguish imprinted on his painted face.

The second brave continued to close and he rose above his pony's head to hurl his lance. Jed tried to steady himself and fired his gun as the approaching brave threw his war lance. He could see that this shot hit the brave above the hip and he shot once more as he saw the lance coming at him. Jed tried to turn unsuccessfully away from the oncoming missile, its impact knocking him backwards to the ground. The second brave then fell into a crumpled ball with the same shocked look, one of his legs breaking on the impact with the ground.

Both horses sped on by as Jed turned on the ground to keep his gun pointed at the motionless and crumpled forms in front of him. A jagged bone protruded through the skin and leathered buckskin leg of the nearest brave as Jed sat with his eyes fixed upon the still twitching bloody leg muscle. He continued to watch as blood begin to spurt forth from around the bone and onto the ground. Only then did he realize that both of the Indians were dead. Thank God for Colt's Walker, was Jed's numb reaction.

Jed sat slumped over, shaking with fear from his narrow escape. His eyes fixed on the two figures who lay sprawled in the dirt. Blood was now coming from the mouth of the second while the first lay face down. As he watched the two dead Indians he slowly attempted to regain control of his own trembling limbs.

Taking deep breaths he began to regain his composure and looked down at the lance impaled in his side. Without hesitating he laid his revolver down and grabbing the lance with both hands gave a quick hard pull. The lance tore loose, pulling and tearing the skin as bright red blood spurted from the wound. He moaned out loud, not from the pain of removing the lance, but from the exertion and pain shooting through his wounded right shoulder.

Holding his left elbow against his stomach he tried to block the blood flow from the serrated wound. Slowly he moved his right hand under the left elbow to hold the skin together. At the same time with his left hand he untied the makeshift sling around his neck. Taking it down, he now wrapped it around his waist and tied the two ends together. Finding that this was not stopping the bleeding, he carefully pulled the wrap around so that one of the knots would seat itself in the wound. This seemed to slow the bleeding. He now took the further luxury of resting to recompose himself.

As he retrieved his pistol and reloaded it he cursed, "Damn it! I knew they would be waiting! So damn close, so damn close."

Jed was somewhat surprised that his adrenaline had kicked in just when he thought he had no more reserves left. Now he rose on shaking and wobbly legs and looked intently about the area. "Did anyone else hear?" The Indian ponies were gone. "They're probably halfway back to Mexico by now," he speculated.

"Peers like somethin', or someone, does not want me going home now. So far it has been one hell'va trip! At least in the army you usually have someone with you for support and backup. Hell, this is getting a mite ridiculous. Clothes in pieces, shot up." He silently wondered what lay ahead.

The seriousness of his close encounter boosted his thoughts to clarity again. He looked to the north. "Not so bad, by three or four days I should be at the river, that is if I can stay alive that long." He remained in this skeptical and cynical mood as he continued to voice the thoughts that came to him.

He looked again at the two bodies from where he stood. They had nothing he could use to help him survive. No water, and that alone would be his salvation. Finally he turned his back on the two Indians knowing the vultures might soon have full stomachs. Fierce, stubborn determination made Jed step smartly again towards his goal of reaching the river. With the river in his possible grasp he now felt better and was more alert.

Midday came and went slowly as he doggedly continued northward. He stopped once to cut open another cactus for whatever slight moisture he could draw from the straw-like pulp. The pain and stiffness of starting out after this stop was excruciating.

There will be no more stops he vowed until reaching water. The effort to start tired muscles was too much to endure repeatedly. Moreover, he could feel blisters starting to form on his feet. The riding boots he was wearing were not the type of footwear for a prolonged hike through the desert.

Again the exertion began to take its toll on his body and mind. He stumbled, he fell. Again and again he willed himself up and to plod onward. Night came and with it moonlight. He continued walking and falling on into the night. Both his strength and reasoning were unstable. He fell. He rested, he slept. He rose and continued on.

Time became a blur. The sun rose and tormented its victim. Jed swore at the sun and the heat. Still his unconscious will forced him onward. The sun finally set. Nighttimes came and passed. He was becoming delirious and dreamed of water gushing down from a waterfall. Still he pushed on towards the water in his dreams. His lips were now swollen, cracked and blistered along with the rest of his face. No longer did he rant and rave. His only unconscious thought was to push on. Slowly another agonizing sun neared the horizon. Mornings came and went.

At times a rational thought came and went as well. He vaguely noticed birds flying high in the sky, possibly heading for their evening drink. The Brazos was surely within reach. It just had to be.

"Smoke!" He could see smoke! With a jolt his mind began to register. He was starting to reason again.

A slight plume of smoke was rising near a grove of cottonwoods along a river bank. He was very sure it was the rest of the war party. Keeping a low ridge between him and the smoke, he veered away and angled toward the river. "Too damn close to take any chances now," he warned himself.

As he cautiously neared the river he became more alert and was determined not to take any unnecessary risks. He could smell the water and although his pace quickened, a clear presence of mind now guided and guarded his every step. He was prepared. He was ready. At last he crept into a smaller copse of cottonwoods further downstream and stepping lightly and cautiously he pushed on towards the river bank. Glancing furtively both left and right he saw that nothing moved. Nothing looked askew. Patiently he forced himself to wait and listen as the sun slowly dipped below the skyline then he slid face first down the short and steep bank to the water's edge and into the water. Quietly he lay and drank his fill of the wonderful lifesaving liquid.

Darkness was now sweeping across the landscape. Jed continued feeding his thirst, while silently and carefully pouring water over his head, neck, wounded shoulder and over his lance wound. Wanting to take no further risks from a possible war party camped up river he climbed back up the bank still taking care to wipe out his tracks as he retreated into the underbrush and away from prying eyes.

He moved his back up against a small cottonwood, his pistol on his lap ready to use if he should hear the slightest noise. Finally comfortable with his limited cover he allowed himself the pleasure of rest and sleep for his fatigued body.

The screech of a magpie awoke Jed with a start!

"Was that a Comanche?" Again he heard the sound of a magpie and his eyes followed the sound. He relaxed slightly as he saw the familiar black and white feathers of the camp robber in a distant tree.

The sun had been up more than two hours. Jed was sheltered from the sun by the foliage of the trees and underbrush slept longer than intended. The water and his achieving the goal of the river made him feel optimistic. He was sure that he could make it home in two more days, possibly three, if he could avoid another war party.

He rose and stood cautiously, turning slowly, as he scanned the surrounding river banks. Only then did he move off carefully and quietly along the upstream bank. "I don't need any more surprises," he continued to remind himself.

Using the trees and ground cover along the bank to prevent being seen, he carefully and methodically made his way along the river's edge. Only two mourning doves noticed him as they gave flight away from this intruder who had spoiled their morning baths. They flew but thirty to forty feet and in watching them Jed realized that there was no one in this immediate area at the moment. Had they flown further he would have suspected that other people were in the area too.

"He had been right! A war party was here last night." He saw the remains of their campfire near the bank and the scattered tracks of their unshod mounts where they crossed the river.

He assumed the war party had waited here for the two braves who had jumped him and it appeared that they decided to push on to their own camp with the bounty they had seized. Besides they probably reasoned there was no cause to be concerned that the two braves had not yet returned. After all their quarry was on foot so they had the advantage. They must have felt that the two braves would soon catch up with the main party, confident and boasting of their conquest.

Nevertheless Jed did not take this supposition to be entirely true. He had been lax before, but not again, as he continually watched for any more signs of the party.

Stiffly he crept along the shore and down to the river's edge, finding an easier route down the bank than the evening before. Protected from view by some tall reed grasses he again drank his fill. Then being as silent as possible he carefully began to wash his torn, sore and ripped body. Taking care he washed away at the cuts, nicks and the scores of pest bites he had endured. Tenderly he lightly scrubbed his shoulder and arm that was trying to heal. The arm did not look good. The swelling and infection had began its relentless assault. His stomach wound looked bad as infection was setting in there as well.

The main trail was now more clearly shown as many wagons, settlers and cattle drives had made the journey to the northwest along the river's edge. This route was obviously still used by the Indians as well evidenced by the fire remains he had seen amid the horse droppings, dust, flies and gnats.

Jed's eye noted the new paw prints from an early morning coyote who had been scavenging for his breakfast in the now abandoned campsite. Now with some rest and after washing in the cold water Jed began to realize just how hungry he was. His thirst had been so overpowering that his hunger pains had been temporary pushed aside.

Thirst quenched, his mind thought only of food. "How long had it been? Four, five, six days?" He lost count. Could he dare risk the sound of gunfire to shoot a rabbit, or perhaps a bird? Probably not yet. "No," he determinedly decided. He could make it further.

Soon the warm early morning sun began to rob him of his remaining strength. It forced him to seek refuge and rest under a large cottonwood whose enormous projecting roots reached down over the bank and into the water below. He now realized that in addition to hunger he was extremely weak from the lack of food. The intense exertion of the past week had taken almost everything out of him. He felt his ribs and thought somewhat sarcastically that he wouldn't even make good vulture bait now.

He rose from under the shadows of the tree and set out again focusing on the Black Pine Mountains in the distance and the thought of the nuts that grew in the pinon trees spurred him on. Just anything to eat was now his goal.

The sun persisted in its relentless assault as Jed's stops for rest and cover become more frequent. Again he moved into the shade of a small sapling and eased himself down against its narrow trunk.

The were no longer any signs of the Indian pony tracks and he felt a bit more confident as he peered from under his sanctuary into the waves of blistering heat rising along the river road. His eyelids began to close as he drifted off into a sleeping stupor. He slept as if in a coma. His body was giving up even if his mind had not realized it. The small black ants that crawled over him were now being ignored as they bit at his exposed and dirty skin. His collapse was finally total.

CHAPTER 3

▼

"Senor, senor, are you okay?"

The voice sounded from far off in the distance as Jed vaguely heard the words. His mind and body successfully pushed this intrusion away.

"Juanita, agua pronto," the old man commanded.

The young woman quickly dropped down from the brown mustang she was riding. As she landed, one hand grabbed the water bag that hung from the saddle horn, her grace and beauty evident even as she rushed to her father's side. She reached out and put her hand on the wounded man's forehead. A fever was very evident. His tattered clothes were worse than those of any poor person she had seen. Dirt so completely covered the cuts, bites and scratches that a good look at his skin was difficult.

Senor Martinez now realized that the man was in a critical situation. He took Jed's legs and straightened them as his daughter helped ease his head and shoulders down upon the ground.

Jed moaned aloud as Juanita grasped his shoulders and pulled his torn and ragged shirt away to see some of the causes for his pain. She noted he had been shot and that the arm was now swollen. Carefully she raised his arm and gasped to herself. The wound on the back of the arm was extremely bloated and dirty and a makeshift wrap was around his waist covering a badly infected hole in his side.

"Papa, your knife."

She reached for the knife. Without taking time for anything else she cut into the already taut skin of his swollen upper arm and a torrent of excrement burst forth from the wound. The only good thing she noticed was that there was little sign of blood poisoning, but even so the man was close to dying. She remembered her cousin Miguel who died of blood poisoning and recalled there seemed to be no way of reversing it.

"Mi Dios!" She did not know if they could save him. "Only the Almighty could decide."

She used her fingers to work the infected mass out of the back of his arm. Then while the arm was still draining she carefully removed the rest of the bloody and ragged shirt sleeve exposing the wound on the top of his shoulder. Slowly too, she peeled away the dirty filthy portion of the tattered wrap around his waist. As she pulled it loose the thick dirty encrusted scab broke loose. Blood mixed with dirt and green ooze flowed from the wound as she began washing and wiping away the dirt and debris from the hole in his side. At last temporarily satisfied with the condition of the stomach wound she went back to cleaning the underside of the arm. It was then she noticed the gunshot wound to the back of his head. After finishing with his arm and shoulder she cleaned the head wound as well.

They tore up one of Juan's faded white shirts and two of their towels to make enough bandage material for his many wounds. After cleaning and wrapping the many lacerations on his upper body she and Juan pulled the ruined boots from Jed's blistered and bloody feet. Many of the blisters had broken and turned into blood as the man had pressed on. After wiping down his feet they stripped off the remains of his clothes and bandaged him as best they could before covering him with one of the bedrolls from the wagon.

His tattered clothes and boots, cut to pieces by the elements, now lay in a heap beside one of the saplings. Beside the pile lay his gun belt and the pistol. Attached to the belt was an empty knife scabbard. The knife evidently lost in the struggle to survive.

Juanita moved back and studied the prone figure. Even cleaned up the man looked very bad. His long black hair was dirty, tangled and shaggy and in need of a haircut, but the crease through his scalp was minor and it had started to heal as hair already had begun to grow back near the opening in the skin. He had evidently lost his hat. His face, sun burnt and unshaven for possibly two weeks left a black coarse uneven beard around blistered and swollen lips. Over his newly bandaged chest lay his still swollen right arm now drained and wrapped, motionless in a new sling draped around his neck. Still he was covered with cuts, scratches and bruises beyond count. The right eye was swollen almost shut as well as being black and blue. What had caused the vast extent of his injuries she could not guess.

She wondered to herself. "What had he been through and what happened? How could he survive? Who was he?" These questions and others came from her innate curiosity.

Juan Martinez tied their horses to a small cottonwood near the river and began to set up their campsite so they could stay near the wounded man. Like his daughter Juanita, he knew they dare not attempt to move him in his present condition. They would have to wait until the fever broke and some of his strength returned.

To keep him cool and shaded they slid Jed onto a bedroll and moved him under the cover of some larger cottonwood trees nearby after which they covered him with a thin blanket to protect from the flies, mosquitoes and other mites. Juanita took a towel to the river's edge, wetting it down, then laid it gently on Jed's head to attempt to break his dangerously high fever. During the rest of the afternoon she continually cooled his towels and remained by her patient.

Juan started a small fire to help keep away the mosquitoes and biting gnats. After the fire was burning well he prepared a thin soup over the hot flames and Juanita attempted to feed Jed a spoonful of the warm liquid without success. She realized that he would not be able to eat anything until he woke up. His breathing was now extremely shallow as he was almost comatose.

They finally rested to take stock of the situation and Juan continued to study the features of the man now in their midst. He was slightly familiar, yet Juan was unable to determine who he was.

Juan's command of English was poor and his ability to read English was slight as well, but he was an intelligent and astute man. Both Juan and Juanita normally spoke English as Juan could see it was the tongue to know if one were to succeed in this newly established Republic of Texas. He spoke broken English but he still thought in Spanish. Only Juanita had a firm grasp of English and was able to think in both languages.

"Do you find sumpthin' 'een hees clothes sayin' who he be?" he asked of his daughter.

"No Papa, there was nothing other than a few Mexican coins, perhaps two or three pesos. That is all."

"Nawthin' 'een hees shirt pockets?"

"No, nothing. Actually the pocket was almost torn off the shirt. It was just barely hanging on."

Juan looked towards the pair of tattered boots, thinking those were probably custom made. What remains shows a touch of fine workmanship, but he has no horse. Perhaps it was a wild one and ran off from him, or perhaps it was stolen, maybe by Indians. And the pistola. He had never seen one of the new Army Colts. He admired the revolver's new style as he picked it up and turned it over in his hands, instantly realizing that the new primer and cap firing mechanism was far superior and faster than the old musket loads. He envied the man lying there for his weapon, wishing that he owned as good a weapon. However, Juan's own code of integrity would never allow him to take the gun as his own.

His cursory search continued. The stomach wound appears to have been made by a Comanche lance or an arrow. Still, he is a fairly young man, and why was he in this area? Was he coming from Mexico? Was he a drifter? If so, where was he going? Suddenly Juan jumped to his feet to get a closer look at the man. "Aha, I theenk I know who the stranger ees!"

"Who Papa?"

"I theenk perhaps it ees Jed Garrett. Maybe two or three years ago he go to fight 'een de war. Now that de war hees over, I theenk he ees Jed and he ees now comin' home!"

"Papa, Si. You are right. I too think he looks familiar but I can not tell. I think I am too close to see him good."

Now sure who the stranger was there was no longer any hesitation to spend as much time as was necessary to try to save Jed's life. Their trip to Austin would have to wait. Both father and daughter's only thought was that of a neighbor and fellow human being in need and they began to set up camp. After the camp was arranged Juan untied the horses from the nearby trees and put hobbles on them so they could feed and water themselves along the river's edge.

It was now late in the afternoon and Juanita continued to apply cold wet towels on Jed's forehead. Besides his shallow breathing only an occasional involuntary muscle tremor gave a hint of life within.

Juan filled the coffee pot with water from the river and put it on the edge of the fire to heat. In their tin food container he found some hot peppers which he tossed into the fire to roast for later.

Leaving the towel on Jed's forehead, Juanita took some flour and thickened a bit of chicken broth into soup for the two of them. Next she added some tortillas filled with refried beans to complete the hasty meal. The coffee water began to boil as Juanita emptied the last of their coffee grounds into the hot water to brew. She knew that coffee was on the list of things to get when they got to Austin.

As the day ebbed Juan surveyed the surrounding area before sitting down and resting his back against the front wagon wheel. The sun was beginning its slow descent behind the rim rocks high above the river. His rifle remained resting across his lap in learned readiness and in a few minutes his daughter brought him a cup of the still steaming coffee. The metal cup was hot to the touch of his lips and mouth as he carefully sipped at the edge of the cup, his black mustache slightly drooping downward as it touched the brew within. The evening darkness now started it's slow creep over the landscape.

"It was a wonderful land. So beautiful and open with freedom on a scale unknown to most men," he thought to himself. "My poorer countrymen in Mexico could never imagine the enjoyment of such a place."

It had now been over twenty years since he and his wife Rosa had originally come to the Texas Territory. Unlike most newcomers they understood why the Indians in the territory were resisting the invasion of settlers onto their lands. The Indians enjoyed a freedom and a way of life that was both refreshing, satisfying and necessary for their society and mores. Their very existence was now being threatened. Juan had mixed feelings as other settlers like him were destroying this traditional culture. He tried to rationalize. This is what all men want. Peace and freedom. "Why must it be so hard?"

Now the 'Anglos' were coming in even larger numbers, moving onto lands that had belonged to Mexico. The very land that earlier had been the domain of the Indian tribes. Slowly over the years Juan began to realize that life had always been a struggle over lands and territories. The quest for furs had now passed. Now it was one last race for the land. And the rules seemed to change as the Anglos fought and killed one another in their struggles for this very ground. It seemed that no one, or nothing, could slow down their relentless attack. More came every year.

His own Mexican land title was no longer valid under the new Republic of Texas law. He and Juanita had been on the way to Austin to obtain a Texas title for the lands they had lived on for the past twenty years. Juanita seemed to understand the changes more easily and it was she who insisted that they travel to Austin to get the new Texas title to their land. Their neighbor, Tom Garrett was going to make the trip also, but at the last minute they decided that Juan could file papers for both of them. In return Tom had said he would check in occasionally with Juan's brother Jose to be sure all was well at their spread.

Juan wanted Juanita along and did not feel comfortable leaving her at home, even though his brother was there to help look after things while they were gone. Furthermore the Indians were becoming bolder and had raided some of the other ranches to the south. Also some of the new white Texans were very crude and violent. "No," he decided. "It was not a place to leave a young senorita."

Juanita wanted to go and he agreed with her, knowing that a young woman must see something of the excitement of the city. He felt that with Tom Garrett's help his brother could take care of things for the two or three weeks they would be gone.

Juan remembered back. It had been very difficult for him to raise a young daughter after his Rosa had died. The pain still lingered as Juan thought back. Rosa endured three to four months of extreme stomach pain before she passed away. The padre had called it something named 'consumption'. Juan had cried that night away, but at the next morning's light Juanita needed tending. At the time she was only five years old and her dependency helped Juan focus as he worked through the clouds of despair and grief.

It was after Rosa passed away that Juan's brother Jose came to help out temporarily. The two brothers worked well together and Jose remained in Texas and, as a way of saying thanks, Juan eventually gave his brother a working interest in the land they now claimed to own.

He recalled too, that about eight years ago the Garrett family moved onto the Black Pine meadows near the middle fork of Brown's Creek adjoining the Martinez' land. Tom and Edith Garrett had two young sons, one about eight or nine, the other approximately three or four years old. Juan's mind reasoned that the man lying close to them was Jed. It must be the older son who had enlisted in the Texas guard a few years ago.

The Garretts' had been a steady and helpful influence in this area of Texas. Juan knew the Garrett family as honest and trustworthy neighbors. Neighbors who could rely on each other for support. When Tom and Edith heard of Rosa's death they came by to help in every way they could. Juan was extremely moved by their generosity and the two families became close over the succeeding years. Edith provided a woman's touch for his daughter when he found himself unable to understand her growing needs. "Si, they ees good people," he mused.

The families helped each other build barns, outbuildings and corrals. They worked the spring and fall roundups together, afterwards branding cattle and the new arrivals. Later in the autumn they cut and stored hay for the wintertime. Their herds were meager in the early years but in the last five years each of their herds had grown to more than one thousand head of cattle and horses. They had done very well.

They pooled their resources and at first sold cattle and a few horses to the Mexican government. However, due to the past years of Mexican and Texan hostilities, they now sold primarily to the Texas militia. This they augmented by occasionally selling or trading stock to settlers moving westward.

Juanita stirred up the fire and sparks shot high into the night air while she returned to the river's edge to retrieve more cool, wet rags and towel remnants to put on Jed's forehead.

"Juanita, you no can do more. Ees' time to rest."

She knew her father was right and reluctantly stretched out full length on her bedroll. The stars were out brightly in the sky and she soon realized that it was later than she thought. Glancing at Jed's feverish form, she closed her eyes to think and unwind. After a long hectic day sleep came quickly.

Juan rose before dawn and added some wood to the dying embers after which he moved the sooty coffee pot into the awakening coals to warm up the coffee from the evening before. The morning activity woke Juanita who yawned and sat up still sleepy eyed.

Seeing her awake Juan spoke. "No change little one," and added, "I theenk we load heem een the wagon and take heem home. I theenk he not stand the heat later een the day. Ees the only thing we can do."

She pulled on her boots and then reached out and touched Jed's forehead. Even though his fever remained they both realized they must try and get him to the doctor in Wedgewood.

"Es verdad, no change," she acknowledged as she straightened up and taking a clean towel and some soap from the wagon moved into the morning shadows of the cottonwood trees to answer nature's call. Afterwards she washed in the cool waters of the Brazos, tossing her long shoulder length black hair back like a spirited filly as she rinsed the soap from her face, neck and arms. Then putting her towel around her neck she gathered up the cool damp towel remnants out of the river to put on Jed.

Coming back into camp she paused alongside the wagon to put one of the wet rags on Jed's forehead to try to cool him down. Juanita next changed the bandages on his arm. The wound at the back of the arm had filled with pus again. Carefully she drained it off and bandaged the arm once more. An inspection of the wound in the side of his lower chest caused her to grimace. It did not appear to have improved during the night. The shoulder, head wound and the other numerous cuts appeared to be holding their own.

Juan meanwhile brought in the horses and tossed the hobbles into the wagon before hitching up the team. Next he tied Juanita's mustang behind the wagon. Their breakfast was over quickly as each knew what needed to be done. Then together, with Juanita at Jed's feet, they loaded him into the wagon. She knew it would be a difficult trip for him lying on the hard wagon floor as she put both of their bedrolls under him then covered him with two brightly colored serapes tucked carefully around his body to try to prevent him from rolling side to side.

Juan looked into the back of the wagon to see if Jed was as comfortable as possible. Going around to the front he climbed up onto the seat and gave a light touch to the reins as they set off for Wedgewood and the Garrett ranch. With luck they hoped to arrive at the town of Wedgewood before evening. Then the doctor could tend to Jed's wounds before continuing on to the Garrett ranch.

Juan's wary eyes watched the range spread out before them with a vigilance brought on by years of survival. It was a natural instinct honed by all who traveled this land. The meek and the ruthless all had to learn these hard lessons of the land. Whether the threat be from the floods, drought, famine, Indians and outlaws, all who survived had to be alert.

Juanita continued to apply wet towel compresses on Jed's forehead as the wagon bounced slowly along the rutted road. She knew too that the water she carried would be tepid by noon, but it still would be wet. Jed's low moans now ceased as his body struggled to live.

They followed the wagon road along the serpentine river as they went west into Grass Valley so named for the wild grass that grew on top of the narrow banks of the river. Black Pine Mountain lay on the opposite bank, at least the slightly graduated slopes of the mountain started there.

The wagon continued to bounce in the ruts of the trail as Juanita tried her best to protect Jed from the jarring ordeal. She put one of their extra blankets between one edge of the wagon and his body and she sat on the opposite side to hold him in place and to protect his battered body from the jousting.

No change in the fever. It just would not break. His chances she realized, were slim at best. He did not look like the Garrett boy anymore. Oh, it was he, she was sure. But this was a man, not the scornful and headstrong teenager who had often regarded her with contempt as they grew up on their respective ranches.

How long had it been since she had seen him? One, two years? Yes, two, at least. She had been only fifteen or sixteen at most. Oh, how we change. Her heart ached for him and all his many wounds. As she watched his battered body in it's life and death struggle she realized that there was a rugged handsomeness that was now weather hardened by the elements.

As she changed the cloths she continued to wonder about the man. What had he done? What had he been through? Where was he going? Was it home? What had he seen? How had he changed? The questions tumbled forth but no answers were forthcoming from the mute form that she trying to protect from further pain.

They hurried the team as much as possible with it's wagon load of critical cargo along the narrow road which meandered beside the waterway and finally up the rolling draws towards Wedgewood. Slowly the town's familiar sights came into view.

The new church with its steeple and bell tower appeared first. As the dusty road turned down the main street the rest of the town came into view. First came Hank's Grocery and Hardware, then Brown's yardage store which also sold seed to the ladies for their flower gardens. Early every spring Mister Brown sold garden seed as well to those so inclined to work vegetable plots to supplement their meaty diets.

Opposite Brown's was the Pine Mountain Saloon and next to it Clara's Hotel. The hotel was adequate, but the four room facility was sparse even by Wedgewood's standards. It only had the basic rudiments, a bed, wash pan and a communal outhouse behind the building. Beside the modest hotel was the New Republic Bank just being built. It was owned by newcomers to the town, Robert Blankenship and his wife Betty.

Sam's Restaurant, a greasy hash house, lay kitty-corner across the street from the new bank. Further down the thoroughfare was the Mountain Harness Shop with a lean-to living quarters built on in back. Here were the offices of both Doc Winters and the shop owner 'Big Ed'. Ed had the misfortune to be handed the moniker of 'Big' due to his less than five foot diminutive stature and it had followed him during his forty some years. Beyond the lean-to in back was a small corral for the transient stock.

Juan turned the team and wagon past the church and urging the team on he rolled down the dusty roadway finally pulling up in front of the harness shop. The spry Juan dropped down from the wagon and shouted at Big Ed.

"Senor Ed, Doctor Winters, come queek! I have, I theenk, Mister Garrett's son hurt bad een de wagon."

At that moment Big Ed took the set of tongs in his hands that was holding a bright glowing red horseshoe and turning he dropped the shoe into a nearby bucket of water. The water immediately started to steam and sizzle as if in a volcanic cauldron. Running over to the wagon with his short, quick steps, he peered inside, looking past Juanita who was still trying to protect the limp form.

"That's not, not Garrett's son," he stammered.

"Oh yes, et ees Senor. Eet ees Jed, no James. I find him collapse on Rio Brazos. Senor Doctor, help, queek."

The din out front was enough to alert Doc Winters and he came out of the harness shop through one of the large barn doors and moved quickly towards the wagon while asking, "What's the trouble Juan? I heard all this commotion."

"Senor Doctor, ees bad. Senor Garrett's son. Thee oldest, I theenk, and he ees hurt bad!"

To size up the problem the doctor climbed up into the wagon. It was immediately apparent that what Juan said was true. Checking on the unconscious patient he found practically no pulse and limited breathing.

"Ed, grab his shoulders," he commanded. Doc Winters then lifted Jed's legs as they carefully unloaded Jed's limp body from the wagon.

Together they took him from the wagon and continued straight into the shop, around the hot forge, and into the lean-to living quarters in the back of the building. The first room they entered was the doctor's one room office that also served as his clinic. There they laid Jed on the extra bunkhouse bed that Doc Winters kept set up to care for the town locals, the surrounding ranchers, and the occasional passersby.

Juan and Juanita paused as they were trying to decide what to do next.

"Now we must go back to Austin to get the new land deeds," Juanita reminded her father.

"But who will tell Senor Garrett 'bout hees son? We no leave him alone here," he added.

"He is in good hands with the doctor. I can ride out to the Garrett ranch and tell them. Then I will catch up to you."

As they were deciding what to do, Big Ed came back out of the harness shop and up to the Martinez's wagon. Ed knew that all of the ranchers in this remote area had to re-file for new titles to the property they were presently living on. He was also aware that Juan and Juanita had set off to Austin originally for the purpose of this re-filing.

Hearing their conversation, Big Ed spoke up. "At the moment his recovery is entirely up to the Doc and God. I can ask Clara Dixon to send her cleanup boy from the hotel out to Tom's ranch and let them know what has happened. Because of the time you have lost by doubling back here, why not turn around and continue back on your run to Austin. We can also have someone go out to see Jose just to keep an eye on your place and let him know what happened and that you may be gone a bit longer."

The suggestion made sense to Juan and Juanita and they began preparations again for their trip to Austin.

Such was the fact of new governments. Everything must be witnessed and approved on official papers or land robbers like the Butcher family would quickly steal acreage from under people who hadn't taken time to file or from people who didn't realize that they had to file again.

With their original destination back in mind, father and daughter again set off to retrace their route back towards Austin, comfortable in the knowledge that Big Ed would get word to the Garrett family about Jed as soon as possible.

CHAPTER 4

▼

A blanket of gray and black storm clouds were approaching from out of the Gulf of Mexico and Tom Garrett knew that a rainstorm was on the way. It would be welcome and refreshing, but at the same time it would soon turn the ground into a quagmire of gooey mud. The drag bucket that he was pulling behind the large black work horse would be unworkable in the resulting gumbo. He had been using the drag bucket to scoop dirt from the side of a small slope and then pulling the loaded bucket down to the bottom of the hill. At the bottom of the hill he had been dumping the dirt into the small gorge to form the face of the earthen dam which was to serve as a water reservoir for the livestock. A storm would make the work impossible and accordingly he decided to quit working at the dam site.

"Gee, Blackie," he commanded the horse and as Tom walked beside the drag bucket the animal obediently turned to the right around a mound of exposed rock still pulling the drag bucket behind him. They continued out onto the newly formed dike and emptied the drag bucket.

"Whoa now. Back, back," and again the large black work horse moved back about two steps. Letting the reins drop, Tom moved up and unhitched the drag bucket and the singletree harnessed behind the horse. Free from the load Tom picked up the reins and pulled himself onto Blackie's back setting off for the ranch before the storm hit.

Tom never carried a watch but even so he knew it to be about four in the afternoon. He should arrive at the ranch in approximately thirty minutes, just ahead of the rain. He could use the little rest before milking time to check in on Jed.

Only two days earlier Bobbie Roberts, the Dixon cleaning boy, had ridden out to the Lazy 'G' to notify Edith of Jed's arrival in Wedgewood and the condition he was in. Immediately Edith put aside her chores, hitched Blackie to their old four wheeled wagon and set off for Wedgewood.

In the meantime Doc Winters had finished making a careful check of Jed's condition and was amazed that not one single bone in his body had been broken. As he unwrapped the bandages put on by Juanita he realized that if Jed lived he could credit both Juanita and Juan for their prompt action. He then cleaned Jed's wounds again and had dabbed iodine on many of the cuts on his head, legs, arms as well as the lance wound on his side.

It was shortly after this that Edith arrived. Together they discussed Jed's present condition. There was nothing more that they could now do for the patient other than wait for the fever to break. It was finally decided that Edith could take Jed home, but he warned, "Be sure and change the poultice on his side at least two times a day. That is the most critical thing, 'cause if gangrene sets in it could prove fatal."

When Tom came in from rounding up some strays on the upper pasture Edith had returned to the ranch with Jed lying unconscious in the back of the wagon. With some help from James who had gotten home a bit earlier from the big meadow, they brought Jed into the house and into the bedroom near the back door of the ranch house.

Even though that had been two days ago Edith was still shocked at Jed's unconscious condition. His face remained battered and swollen around his right eye. The total number of cuts, scratches and gashes gave her the impression that he had been dragged behind a horse.

She continued to change Jed's bandages as needed and to apply soothing oils to his ravaged body thus adding moisture to his skin to aid in the healing process. The worst wound appeared to be the puncture on his left side and she changed the poultice made of bread and herbs each morning and evening per Doc Winters instructions. The doctor said that it was deeply infected but the poultice appeared to be drawing out some of the infection. In addition Edith hand massaged the area approximately every four hours to force the wound to bleed and cleanse itself in the bleeding process. As she tended to him she noted the deep lines in his face and realized the war must have been very difficult for him.

There was finally a good sign however. His fever finally began to lessen. At the same time his leg muscles began to twitch and his torso to writhe while he emitted deep low moans. He unconsciously continued his march and struggle to survive while Edith continued to tend to his wounds. In the past two days she was able to get some chicken soup into him, one small spoonful at a time.

Edith heard, then saw, Tom ride Blackie up to the barn. Within minutes Tom unharnessed Blackie and put him out in the corral for the coming evening. Taking a pitchfork from inside the barn door he tossed two shocks of hay over the fence and into the corral feeding trough. After making sure there was water in the water trough he came striding towards the house.

Coming through the front door he asked, "Any change?"

"Yes, I do think he may be coming around. He has been moaning and his arms and legs are starting to jerk like they want to move. I think he is moaning just because everything hurts so bad."

Tom entered the bedroom and peered down upon the figure on the bed. He noted Jed had more color and that too was a good sign.

"Any luck getting any food down him?"

"Just a couple spoonfuls of soup, but that is about all. Though his fever is starting to drop a bit and that's a plus," she added.

Edith rose from the chair beside the bed and went out into the kitchen leaving Tom to study Jed's condition.

Since the advent of the war Tom missed his son immensely and inwardly awaited the few scant letters he sent home assuring them he was alive and well. Painfully both he and Edith had endured his absence. Tom enduring in his stoic silence and Edith openly fretting for his welfare. Just seeing Jed now in this shocking condition worried both of them.

Presently James came into house and asked about Jed. Momentarily satisfied with his mother's reply he dropped into the nearest chair. James too missed his older brother especially because of the added workload thrust upon him, and to Tom's credit, he increased the chores more slowly on James than he had with Jed. Perhaps subconsciously he really understood what had driven Jed away to fight in Mexico and did not want the same strained relationship with his remaining son.

The afternoon wind and rain started as Edith began to prepare the evening meal. Flashes of lightning streaked across the darkened sky and the resulting thunder shook the earth as if to remind mankind who rules the heavens and earth. Later after supper Tom and James, hunched low under their hats to block the rain, ran out to the barn to work on an evening task of repairing Blackie's horse collar which was beginning to fray.

Mornings come alive rapidly on the Garrett ranch. The early morning light set off the roosters in a cacophonic serenade to the early dawn and shortly two Mexican crossbreed cows came towards the barn in readiness for being milked and fed. If left standing for more than an hour or so they would soon start mooing of their discontentment and discomfort.

The mustangs and work horses in the corral slowly ambled down to the watering trough and drink their fill as they looked expectantly for their breakfast. Their pecking order is firmly established. First is Blackie, the ten year old workhorse standing eighteen hands high, commanding and receiving the respect of the younger, smaller mustangs. He is followed by seven year old Jack, then Blondie about the same age. Red, Maggie and her year old foal Turnip, rounded out the mainstay of the small remuda. These horses had become the work core while the rest of the ten or so young mustangs in the corral were in limbo, still a little wild, and as of yet most not named. They were used as needed to relieve the other horses in the roundups and branding or for sale to passing settlers moving west and to the army. On occasion animals belonging to visitors or hired hands would also be in the bunch, like the small all black mustang belonging to the grub line rider who was bedded down in the tiny bunkhouse attached to the right of the barn.

The adobe ranch house sat with its front porch facing the morning sunrise. Edith enjoyed the first light of the morning coming in fresh and pure. In the warm evenings, when time, chores and weather permitted, Tom and Edith would relax in the welcome shade the porch provided. It was a special place too, to spend with neighbors or other travelers who might pass by.

Less than a quarter of a mile behind the house was Crow Mesa rising up some two hundred feet into the sky. The name was obvious as above the summit one could usually see the black outlines of the crows as they circled high above the butte.

Stirring came from the ranch as evidenced by a wisp of smoke coming from the chimney. First Edith checked in on Jed and seeing no immediate change she began to prepare breakfast for the men. While Edith fixed the morning meal James went out to milk the two milk cows. Tom too was busy with the morning chores as he went to the barn to feed and water the animals and then to check on the new man.

Cob Davenport was the new hand. He was a grub line rider, a rover, like many of the men who traveled alone. While others sometimes teamed up with a fellow traveler they all went from ranch to ranch working here and there. These wanderers generally came from the eastern states to Texas on their way to where, they knew not. Since the war was over more men were on this circuit working for first one spread and then another as they moved along in life. Most had two good qualities. They would work cheap for their keep and they brought welcome news from other parts. Usually the news was grossly exaggerated but still there was always enough truth to the various stories that circulated to provide a basis of fact for the tales. One just had to know how much to believe.

Unlike the immigrating eastern seaboard grub line riders, Cob came down the Mississippi River from St. Louis, the jumping off spot for the west. His father worked in a hardware store that outfitted many of the wagons moving westward and the abundant tales of adventure were responsible for prompting his zest for travel and excitement. At eighteen years of age he was six feet tall and already had the physical body to withstand the rigors of many hours work. Finally, unable to contain his energy and wanting to search for his dreams, he had signed on as a boatman to help bring a load of furs down to New Orleans. When the trip was completed it seemed only natural to take his wages and buy a horse and saddle and head out in a westerly direction. He moved slowly through the Arkansas Territory and into Texas working at various ranches along the way and became, over time, a competent and dependable ranch hand. Twelve years had rapidly passed by. He had no desire to return to St. Louis, the cold winters did not beckon to him. He was calm and serene, satisfied to receive an occasional letter from his parents each year and to enjoy the people he met in his travels. His needs were few and he liked it that way. Lines of confidence became etched in his face, most earned from the many hours he spent in the outdoors.

He seemed to hit it off right away with the Garrett family. Tom was only some ten years older and they got on well over the past two months and respected each other's opinions. James, on the other hand, possibly in the exuberance of youth could be a little hot headed at times. Still they gave him consideration and respect. He, in turn, gave them his labor willingly. Besides that it was nice to live in a bunk house again, be out of the elements and to have some home cooked meals. At least for a while.

He shuffled out of the bunkhouse into the bright morning sun to join Tom and James. Soon all three came into the house and sat down for breakfast. While they ate they discussed the day's work.

"I'm goin' to harness Blackie and go down to see if I can finish the dam today," Tom said as he drank down the last of his coffee. "James, why don't you take Cob, and you two ride the south range around the big meadow and start to pushin' the cattle back this way. We've lost too many to rustlers and Indians this year."

"Yeah, and that Butcher bunch has been responsible for the most of it," replied James. "They've been pushing their cattle over onto our pasture and watering their herd from our dams."

The Butcher family came to the Black Pine Mountain area over four years ago and purchased the old Johnson place that lay to the east of the town. Ben Johnson had worked the section of ground for eight years, and after the death of his wife, he took the first offer on the property. In the past four years the Butchers added to the old homestead in more ways than one. New and larger barns had been built as well as a bigger bunk house for the ranch hands. Their herds of cattle grew surprisingly fast and many of the old timers suggested that the Butchers were not above branding any cattle as their own, even if they knew better. Also was the fact that some of the hands they hired were handier with their guns than with the usual tools of cattle ranching.

"Well don't start any problems if you should see any of their men. I plan on talking to some of the neighbors, then we will take a ride over and see if we can talk some sense to Clyde Butcher," Tom continued on, "but I want to wait 'til Juan Martinez gets back from Austin. Then we'll get together with all the rest of the ranchers before we have our little talk with him."

"From what I've heard he doesn't pay much attention to anyone anyway. We already know that he has taken some of our yearlings and put his brand on them," snapped James as he reached for another piece of fried ham.

"Look, with all the cattle presently running wild and loose in this country it can happen if we don't get them branded before they are weaned from their mothers, so we can't be too critical."

"Even so they keep getting pushier and pushier. He moved in and took over the Jacobs' place and he had over one thousand acres, or thereabouts."

"Jus' don't look for trouble," ordered Tom firmly. "We don't need to start up any range war."

With that said the men finished up the last of the coffee as they rose to pursue their jobs for the day. As they went out the door each took a lunch that Edith had packed for them. Inside each of the cloth lunch bags she put strips of beef jerky, two hard rolls with apple butter, two hard boiled eggs and one of the late fall apples from their small orchard out back which consisted of twelve assorted fruit trees.

With the men out from underfoot Edith busied herself with the cleanup of the morning dishes as she poured some hot water from the kettle on the stove into the cold water in the sink. She stood washing the cookware as the men left to do their respective tasks. Still she was troubled by this morning's conversation concerning the encroachments, mainly by the Butchers. Other land grabbers too had moved into the area but none of the others were quite as aggressive.

She was suddenly startled from her thoughts by a groan from Jed in the back bedroom. Turning towards the sound she dropped the dishrag on the floor as she hurried into the room.

Jed opened his eyes and looked around the dimly lighted room. "Where.., where?" was the stammered question.

"Don't worry, everything's okay." she assured him. "Just lay back and rest. It's all over. You're home."

Jed's mind reeled as he began to realize he was safe. "Mother?", he spoke as his eyes slowly began to focus about the room. "Home.., home, I don't believe it! How did I get here? When did I get here?"

Try as she might Edith was unable to get Jed to rest. He tried to raise himself, but quickly lay back down on the bed. His body hurt everywhere. Resolutely he finally lay still, resigned at least for the time being. Still the questions tumbled forth, slowly at first, than more rapidly as he regained strength and became more aware of his surroundings.

Edith began to answer his questions, slowly explaining how the Juan and Juanita found him by the river and brought him to Doc Winters in Wedgewood. All that she knew of she patiently explained. As she filled in the blanks, Jed became aware of his intense hunger and asked for something to eat. Quickly she tossed more wood in the kitchen stove and reheated the chicken soup she had been attempting to feed him before. She added two slices of fresh baked bread and butter to the tray as she took it into the room. With Edith's help he ate. Then he lay back, closed his eyes and slept, but not before she changed the bandage covering the wound on his side.

About eleven in the morning Jed awoke again. He tried to remain quiet and get up but quickly realized he was far too sore to go moving out of the bed for the moment. He rested some more and soon was able to get up to a sitting position. Within an hour he was able to stand up and hobble on his blistered feet into the living room where he sunk down in Tom's large rocking chair, physically spent. It was here that he spent the remainder of his first waking day.

Jed spent the next few days trying to fill in the lost pieces of his memories while at the same time rapidly regaining his strength. His right eye was still black and blue although the swelling had gone down. His face itched from his still somewhat matted black beard adding to his battered overall appearance. The rest of his face, although covered with many welts and nicks, improved enough that he eventually managed to shave. The stiffness began to ease from his joints as he slowly began to move about more and more.

He requisitioned some of James's and his father's clothing as his own was too tattered to be of any practical use. Hobbling about in his dad's boots required at least two extra pairs of socks but he had no choice as his own custom made boots were totally destroyed.

When the family gathered Jed explained and answered questions about his trip home. He outlined the puzzling ambush and his being tracked by the Indians, but he held back talking about the actual Indian attack by the two braves on his arduous walk to the river. It made Edith and Tom realize that they were extremely fortunate to get their son back alive and both knew they owed a large debt of gratitude to Juan and Juanita.

One evening after dinner as the family, including the extra man Cob, were sitting on the front porch the subject of the conversation turned to horses. Jed mentioned that on his trip home he lost his large brown roan with white on the tips of his ears. As he described the horse Cob inquired, "White on the ear tips you say?"

"Yeah, a little unusual, but you couldn't miss him among the other horses," was Jed's reply.

"Ya' know, I saw one jus' like that 'bout a week ago. Saw this guy headed west towards the Colorado territory on a big brown roan with white ear tips. Said he'd jus' bought her from some feller who said he needed the money."

"Could very well have been the one I had. Sure sounds like it anyway."

"Hey boys," said Tom cutting in. "Tomorrow one of us should ride over to the Martinez place. I promised Juan that we would check in from time to time with his brother Jose." Tom also felt it was time that Jed get some of the soreness worked out of his body when he ordered, "Jed, saddle up Maggie and take her out for the day over to Juan's and check things over." As an afterthought he added, "We need to get her away from that colt of hers anyway."

The slightly veiled harshness of the order bit, but Jed quietly replied, "Sure. I'm about to go stir crazy settin' 'round here doing nothin'. When do you expect them to be back?"

"Probably won't be back for another couple of weeks or longer. It's a long way down to Austin and back with a wagon. I was going to go myself but then Juan felt his gal needed to see some of the big city."

"And he is right," said Edith. Knowing that Juan could only read and speak Spanish well she added, "She can help with reading and writing in English. Besides, a young girl needs to get out and see what is happening in the world."

"And he is going to get some supplies for us as well," Tom added. "He's also re-filing for me since we had that big land change making Texas a territory now.

He may just end up bringing me the papers to be filled out and sent in. We'll have to wait and see."

"Well, I've got to get some shuteye tonight if I'm goin' to ride tomorrow," Jed put in as he rose, and opening the screen door, stepped into the house. The slam of the screen door signaled an end to the gathering and shortly thereafter the rest of the group on the porch broke up, each to take care of any personal duties before retiring for the evening.

The next morning as Jed was in the barn putting the saddle on Maggie, James came into the barn with a small sack lunch lunch and Jed's gun belt complete with his Colt. "I thought you might like this," he remarked as he handed both over to Jed. "I took the gun apart and cleaned it for you. It sure is one fine gun."

Jed's gaped in amazement. "I.., I thought it was gone," he gasped. "I lost everything else and I assumed that it was gone too. I really want to thank you for cleaning it all up." A large smile of appreciation spread across Jed's face as he mounted up and stood in the stirrups while belting on the holster, then tying off the leg strap.

"I took the knife scabbard off the belt since there was no longer a knife in it. Left it in your room up on the hat shelf." James continued, "I've only seen one gun like it and that is owned by Eddie Swanks. Claims he bought it off of a passing settler, but I doubt it. 'Mebbe you'd let me try it out. I've never shot one of those Colt repeater's before."

"Well, not now. I've got to get going to the Martinez place so I'll see you later. We'll do a little practice when I get back in."

Happy with Jed's answer James added, "I put the powder and the patches and balls along with a few of those copper primin' caps in your saddle bag. See ya' later." With that exchange James turned and went to help Cob in the barn.

Jed gently touched Maggie's ribs with his heels and they moved off down the worn path and proceeded south alongside Crow Mesa butte. The morning sun felt warm and comfortable on Jed's face as he looked forward to the ride. The creak of the saddle and the smell of the leather, mingled with the aroma of the sage and the familiar landscape all helped to offset the occasional pains left over from his harrowing trip home. At last his stomach wound began to heal over. The wounds to his head and shoulders were feeling much better too. Only the pain from his once blistered feet was especially noticeable and he had taken a special effort before leaving the house to put on two pairs of thick wool socks before slipping on his father's large, well worn boots. He pulled down the brown old western hat on his forehead he had borrowed from James. As he moved out he was finally content with the world.

Riding along leisurely, he pulled his Colt Walker from the holster and nodded approvingly at the cleaning job James had done. Both the inside and outside of the weapon had been cleaned and oiled. Satisfied, he put four powder wads in four of the cylinders, added the lead slugs then pulled the seating rod down to en-bed the loads. Next he carefully seated four caps at the other end of the cylinders. The fifth and last cylinder he left empty for the hammer to rest on. It was too dangerous to let the hammer rest against a live cap. He remembered army friends of his who had been severely wounded and some crippled by accidental firings.

After three hours the terrain began to level out as he proceeded south. Coming to Flat Creek, a small tributary of the Brazos, Jed stopped to allow Maggie to drink. He dismounted and moved upstream to quench his own thirst rather than drink the warm water from the water bag tied to his saddle horn.

Mounting up again he continued across grassy prairie. An occasional gust of wind made the grasses ripple in front of him as he rode. He knew both the Garrett and the Martinez families were fortunate to have grazing land as good as this. It could support thousands of cattle and for that reason alone many new settlers were coming from the east to stay in Texas.

The news of the rich Texas grasslands was spreading rapidly across the country enticing more and more settlers. Many of these new arrivals did not understand that this was no longer open range to be shared by all as the choice land had already been claimed and filed for by families like Martinez and the Garretts. As a result the present land owners had to constantly be on the alert for squatters, land thieves and rustlers. It had become a time of unrest. Owners began to band together to protect their holdings. At the same time new and unscrupulous men were buying up some of the poorer ranches whose owners became disillusioned. Small scale range wars over the land were already occurring further to the south.

In the southern part of the territory the Texas Rangers quickly dealt the law out to those who infringed upon the status quo. In the north, where the law was practically nonexistent, the situation was slowly coming to a head. The town of Wedgewood had not progressed to the point of hiring a sheriff. Nor had one been needed up to this point.

Many people were passing through the area now. The rumors of free land caused an excitement to grip the poor, the homeless and the unemployed from the war. With great enthusiasm vagrants, trail bums, families, gamblers, entrepreneurs, gun fighters, thieves and others with ideas of making quick fortunes in rumored gold were going west. Some were headed for the Great Northwest. Still others were moving on to California. The unrest made Jed realize things had been getting worse during the time he had been gone.

Now ahead, just as the noonday sun reached its highest point, Jed could make out the roof line of the Martinez spread nestled among a stand of cottonwood trees. Juan Martinez too, had chosen his land well. Behind the home was a small stream large enough to supply water for the ranch needs year around. Beyond the stream the grass-covered prairie rose gradually towards the south.

As he rode in a dog began to bark a warning and a man wearing a sombrero stepped through the front door with a rifle in hand. "Hold it right there Senor. What do you want?" he inquired.

"Hey Jose, I am Jed Garrett from next door. I just rode over to see how you are making out while Juan and Juanita are gone. Is everything okay?"

"Perhaps, I don't know. Come een and set down. We can talk. I.., I'm sorry I did not recognize you. Yes, please Senor, come and set down," was his confused answer.

To calm the man's apparent fears, Jed moved slowly as he climbed down from the saddle and tied the Maggie's reins to the rail posts in the front yard. Seeing no obvious danger Jose lowered his rifle as he motioned to Jed.

"Come, over here een the shade," he said pointing to three old unpainted wooden chairs under the large cottonwood tree in the front yard.

"Do you want some water, Senor?"

"Maybe later, thanks"

The lean, black bearded Mexican leaned his rifle against one of the chairs as he wearily sat down. The large brown, mixed breed dog, moved beside Jose's chair and lay down by his master while continuing to keep his wary eyes on the stranger. As Jed walked over under the shade of the cottonwood tree he could see the man relax somewhat, but clearly something was bothering him. Easing himself down in the remaining chair, he asked again, "Is everything okay?"

"Not so good," was the slow reply. "Yesterday I was at the big meadow, near I theenk, where your ground meets this rancho. I went to get some strays and bring them back to this rancho. I see other cows marked with a large 'B'. I know that they belong to the Butcher rancho and I start to push them back towards the Butcher ranch. Senor, there was perhaps two hundred cows. Then a man hollers. He was on a brown horse behind some small trees."

Clearly Jose was very nervous and anxious to tell the story. He continued, "I do not see him before. He say to leave theese cows and go. I say no, and he pulls out his rifle and shoots. I turn when he shoots and he hits my horse. I try to ride, but after a short distance, maybe a half mile, the horse dies. I have to walk back to this ranch. I am very worried."

"Have you been back there to see if they are still there?"

"No Senor, not yet. I had saddle another horse, and I was goin' to see jus' as you come. I theenk that you might be one of them. I am very worried."

"Well, together we can ride out and see what's happening," replied Jed. "Two heads are better than one in this case, but let me water my horse first. Have you eaten?"

"Si Senor, I jus' finish."

"Good. Then as we ride along I can eat my lunch. You can show me where it happened and we'll see what is going on."

Obviously relieved to have some help Jose rose from the old dilapidated chair he was sitting on. The dog slowly moved out of the way while Jose retrieved his rifle leaning against the other chair.

Quickly the two men made themselves ready while Jose packed extra food, water and ammunition just in case. Jed watered Maggie and after checking his pack for his food and water, stepped up into the saddle, his hand instinctively touching his Colt to assure himself of it's readiness. No conscious thought was made. The touch was all reflex. His mind was already preparing for what might lie ahead.

As they rode towards the meadow that Jose had described each man was concerned with what could happen. Jed ate his lunch he continued to question Jose about yesterday's happenings to glean out all the details. He wanted no unexpected surprises. Jose could not say if there were more than one person. They would have to wait and see.

Before long they could see the land curve in the distance down into the area both families knew as 'the meadow'. It was not overly distinctive from the rest of the area. Its only real determining difference was that it naturally fell off into a large meadow where the grass grew more lush and there was a year around pond of water in the center, a donation of nature that both ranches had shared over the years.

Cautiously they rode closer. Jed realized that Jose might not be as capable as he, but he could be an asset.

Jed reined to a stop. "Jose, you go 'way 'round to the left. Try to keep as much of the hill between you and Butcher's herd as you can. Take off your hat, and just barely look over into the meadow. Do not go any further until you see me moving into the meadow from here. Comprende?"

"Si, yes."

"After you see me riding in, wait until I meet up with Butcher's men. Then you ride in closer with your rifle ready, but do not come down into the meadow," he commanded. "Only ride in a short way. Wait with your rifle up on the edge of the meadow to shoot if I need help. Okay?"

Jose's weapon was actually an old single shot Mexican style musket, but from a distance one could not tell, and that's what Jed was banking on.

"Si senor. I will do it."

Jose turned his mount obediently and moved at an angle towards the western side of the meadow. Jed sat watching Jose ride up the back side of the shallow hillside. He needed to wait to allow him time to get into position. Jed's plan was simple. Since he probably had the advantage of the repeating Colt's rapid fire power he would ride straight into the camp, hoping that there were not more than a couple of Butcher's men there. His experience from the Mexican War made him realize that sometimes a direct frontal attack can work the best.

After Jose disappeared from view Jed nudged Maggie and slowly began riding deeper into the meadow land. A thin wisp of smoke rose off to the right of the center of the low plain and he made straight for the campsite near the pond, his adrenal glands making him alert to every sound and move. He could see the herd of about two hundred head of longhorns grazing on the lush grass north of the campsite.

Closer to the camp he could make out two horses and nearby two men lying down as if having a noon siesta. He drew the Colt Walker and rested it in plain view on his lap as he advanced. Looking left he noted that Jose was moving into position up on the ridge line, his musket pointing into the air with it's butt resting on the front of his saddle.

Suddenly becoming aware of Jed's approach the two men scrambled to their feet. The taller of the men, wearing a large black hat, reached for his rifle as the other retrieved his hat from the ground and hurried towards their horses.

Jed continued his slow and steady approach. The man with the rifle was unshaven and dirty in appearance. Both men gave the impression of rustlers, or perhaps in this situation, hard case trail bums working for Butcher. Jed watched too, as the shorter man moved to the horses and stood waiting with one hand holding onto a saddle strap.

Jed did not hesitate as he continued to advance and as he moved closer he said firmly, "I'm Jed Garrett and I think you boys might be lost."

"Well, I don't give a damn who you are and we ain't lost!" was the reply of the man with the rifle. Then he saw the Colt repeater in Jed's hand and knew instantly he could be at a disadvantage against this new gun. He had only seen one before and that was owned by Eddie Swanks.

"Let me explain it to you," Jed continued slowly. "I've got men all around this meadow and they all have rifles pointed this way."

Both men glanced around and they could see Jose on the hill to the west. Then they furtively eyed the surrounding grassy plain for others as Jed reined Maggie to a stop.

The taller man, backing down and knowing they may be at risk, spoke up, "Maybe we ain't exactly at the right spot, but this is where Clyde Butcher said for us to feed and water this herd. Said this is his land too."

"Boys, this land belongs to the Martinez and the Garrett ranch. I suggest you jus' mount up and start heading those cattle back to Butcher, or we'll stampede the whole damn bunch out of here. And don't forget to tell Clyde he owes us for a dead horse."

Jed said this knowing that the men had better not return without the herd to Clyde Butcher. It was said that Clyde was mighty hard on his people and he was sure they would not dare risk losing the herd and then face his temper as well.

"Okay, but you ain't heard the last of this. Clyde's going to be awfully mad and we don't know nuttin' about a dead horse neither," the man protested as he began to back-peddle knowing that they had lost the dispute. "We'll go, but we'll be back," he warned. "Come on Larry," he snapped at his partner. "Let's get the hell outta' here!"

Their horses moved impatiently as the two men reached for the saddle horns and stepped up into the saddles. The one who had been doing all the talking looked like a dark angry cat that had lost its prey and was snarling at its enemies. They proceeded towards the herd as Jed watched unmoving on his own horse. Slowly and grudgingly they began to move the cattle to the north on a line towards the Butcher ranch.

Jed continued to watch as they disappeared from sight. Only then did he wave Jose in and step down from his horse. As Jose began to ride in Jed walked up to the remains of the campfire and pushed dirt on the small hot embers with his boot edge as little black curls of smoke still rose in the air.

As Jose rode in he remarked, "I don't know what you say to them, but I glad to see them go."

"Just a little bluff, Jose. Just a little bluff and it worked this time. Next time we won't be so lucky. Now let's look for any strays of yours that still might be around here and get them back to your hacienda."

They spent most of the rest of the afternoon rounding up strays in the draws surrounding the meadow pastureland. They found nine cows all belonging to Martinez, six of which had young unbranded mavericks trailing their mothers. Satisfied that they had all the strays they herded the group back to the Martinez ranch. It had been a long day, longer than Jed had anticipated. So saying his 'goodbyes' to Jose and promising to check back soon, he left the still somewhat worried Jose.

By the time Jed reached the Garrett ranch nightfall was starting to descend. First things first, he unsaddled Maggie, quickly rubbed her down a bit and put her out into the corral with the other horses. After making sure there was water and feed he made his way towards the house while massaging his tender left side. Just then James came out of the house.

"'Bout time you got back. What took you so long?"

"Tell you about it inside. First let me wash up and I'll be right in. It's a long story," was Jed's reply.

The rest had finished eating earlier but Edith saved a plate of leftovers from their meal. "It's still somewhat warm so you'd better eat now before the food gets any colder," was her admonishment.

Jed hungrily wolfed down the food and related the story of what had taken place at the meadow. As he spoke the silence of the others permeated the room. All of them knowing that possible trouble lay ahead—trouble that they long hoped would never occur.

Finally Tom spoke, "We must not jump to wild conclusions. Butcher may just back off knowing that we called his hand."

"No, he will be back with the Swank brothers riding out for him to do his dirty work," countered James. "That whole bunch seems to be just spoiling for a fight and I say let's give it to them!"

"Only if they push the issue. But for the time being jus' let things lie," Tom answered.

The debate continued as Edith cleared the table and finished the cleanup of the evening meal. At times their voices were raised in loud concerns. Eventually they all became calm as reason gradually penetrated the discussion.

Finally Cob, who felt he was somewhat of an outsider to the family, excused himself and retired to his small bunk room out by the barn. At that point the rest of the family, tired and weary of the discussion, also retired for the night.

CHAPTER 5

▼

The next few weeks passed peacefully for the two homesteads and no more encroachments were noted by either the Martinez or Garrett families. All the ranchers, large and small, reputable or questionable, were forced to prepare for winter. Of these facts there was no denying so the usual late summer chores were being done with a view to the fall roundup.

Some of the big meadow's lush grass would have to be cut and brought in as winter hay for the livestock. Cattle would have to be brought down from the higher country for the winter. Any calves missed for branding in the spring roundup must be branded at that time and other cattle that had strayed from the neighboring ranches would be herded back to their rightful owners. In a few cases if the animals strayed many miles they would stay on the adopted range until the spring when they would be returned.

This type of cooperation had been the unwritten law of the cattlemen, but it too was changing. This change was caused by the greed of some of the owners of the large spreads who were concerned with making money even if it meant filching cattle from their neighbors. In addition some of these ranches were managed by rough uncompromising men for absentee owners further contributing to the problem.

It had been three weeks since the Martinez' family left and the Garretts were beginning to expect Juan and Juanita back from Austin anytime but no one was worried as everyone realized it normally took about three weeks to make the round trip via wagon.

The days passed and Jed's wounds slowly mended. Only the old lance wound was a little tender from time to time, and it was kept in this state from the continual jarring in the saddle as he made the rounds with Cob and James as well as riding over to check on the Martinez place.

As he gained in strength Jed began to grow restless and he puzzled over the reason. Somehow he was not comfortable. He knew he was finally at home, but none the less he began to fret. He thought of the friends he had left in the army, more specifically, the Rangers that he had ridden with. Slowly he began to realize that yes, home was wonderful to come back to, but he was beyond that now. He would ultimately have to leave again. He must look for his own future, whatever it may be. He decided to help finish the fall roundup before telling his family of the decision he had made.

With his mind finally becoming more at ease he decided to take a ride into Wedgewood to see what new things had been added to the town during his absence. On the following Saturday morning, after Edith insisted he take some money from the ranch funds, he made a list of things he needed like shirts, pants, new boots, ammunition and a new hat before riding off to town.

Riding along he began to mentally reminisce about trips he had taken to town as a young boy. The pleasure and the excitement he experienced jumped again to his mind. The trips were normally made to buy supplies or to bring livestock in to be sold. Sometimes they traveled to town to buy a good bull or a fine piece of horseflesh and these times were normally more festive. The ladies would prepare a picnic lunch to be shared with other families in the area as they gathered for the occasion. All were scrubbed, combed, coiffured and dressed in their finest attire. The older folks gathered to catch up on news from near and far, on family, friends, crops, weather, cattle and livestock prices. Gradually the conversations expanded to include local and territorial politics, Indian raids, and legal problems and many opinions were tossed back and forth.

The younger boys, including Jed, would gather to play games and show off for the young girls who pretended not to notice. Becky and Betty Ann Jacobs were two of the more attractive girls the boys all tried to impress. Then there was the Brown family who lived way north of town and had two boys and three girls.

"Let's see, there was Tommy, Larry, SueAnn, Roberta, and what was the other girl's name? Can't think of her name now," he pondered. He realized it was now doubtful any of those young ladies were still in the area or even available.

Wedgewood was certainly not like some of the cantinas along the border where anything was available as long as the pesos lasted. Tequila, rum, whiskey, along with many brands and qualities of Mexican beer, or cervesa, was convenient for the asking, plus there were senoritas with long, black hair and flashing, dark enticing eyes to tempt and help wile away hot passionate nights. Sedate

Wedgewood could hardy compare to that kind of sensual excitement. Still it would be nice to see his home town again and note the changes. The warm sun on his shoulders enhanced the ride and his thoughts as he cantered along.

Soon the spire of the new Methodist Church became visible. The church construction was started by the local Methodists who had moved into Wedgewood some six years ago but it wasn't until Reverend Baker came to town that real progress on the project was apparent. The Reverend was from either Tennessee or Kentucky and not too much was known of him. It was rumored that he was run out of one of those states and had moved on to Texas. Some said it was over money, others said it was because of a woman, and still others said he had killed a man. It might have been all three reasons, but regardless, Reverend Baker was the man most responsible for the new building.

He passed by and rode slowly into the town. Next he saw Hank's Grocery and Hardware with its familiar wooden walkway in front covered protectively by a sloped wooden roof. A wooden bench sat underneath next to the building where shoppers and neighbors often sat in the shade offered to discuss local issues of the day.

He felt pleased that between Hank's Grocery and Brown's yardage store he was able to get the list of items he required. Then tying his bundled purchase behind his saddle he rode up the road to Sam's Restaurant where he dismounted, and tossing a quick wrap of the reins around the hitching rail, walked inside.

The place hadn't changed one bit. Five tables and chairs were arranged on the left side of the room as he entered. At the back on the right hand side of the room was a short swinging door that opened into Sam's kitchen. The appetizing aromas that filtered throughout whetted his appetite as Jed made his way to a vacant table in the far left corner. Only one of the other tables was in use and that was occupied by two of the local ladies who were busying themselves in the current town gossip while they looked out the window.

Jed eased himself down on one of the hard wooden backed chairs. Facing the street he stretched his legs out under the small table to get as comfortable as possible. On the far wall near the kitchen door hung Sam's menu which was printed on a large piece of faded butcher paper. 'Stew', 'Man Sized Steaks', 'Lady's Steaks' and, 'Fried Chicken' were the offerings of the day. And even though the menu never varied much, Sam did have a reputation for clean food at fair prices that allowed him to eke out a meager living from the local citizenry.

A strawberry blond haired waitress came out of the kitchen. "Hello ya'all", was the cheerful greeting. "Ya'all figured out what you'd like?"

"Yes, let's try the stew, and a cuppa' black coffee to go with it," he added.

"Anything else?"

"No, not now."

With that she turned and smiled, perhaps a bit more than to some of the other customers who came through the door.

He eyed her closely as she turned and went back into the kitchen to place his order. She had to be new to area because he was sure he would have remembered her. She had long strawberry blond hair, just slightly longer than shoulder length, and a very pleasant long torso which hinted of slender long legs under her floor length light blue skirt. His thoughts continued to admire the young woman as he gazed around the plain room.

An old dusty painting of a vase containing large white petaled flowers was the only adornment on the wall opposite Sam's menu. The remaining white thinly painted walls were showing grime from the dust of the street and the grease from the kitchen that permeated the building over the years.

The ladies at the front window were still busy in their gossip and they paid little attention to the stranger in the back of the room. The focus of their conversation was on the people who rode or walked by on the street in front of the building.

The waitress returned with his coffee. "Sugar, Sugar?" she asked trying to entice Jed somewhat.

"No thanks. Never use it." He purposely passed over the slightly veiled lure that she had offered.

With that she turned and busied herself in her duties as she went to assist the ladies in the front of the cafe. Then she wiped off two of the wooden tables and rearranged the few chairs around them before going back into the kitchen.

Presently she returned with a large steaming bowl of the house stew and set it before him. "Holler if ya'all want sumpin' else," was her quick reply as she went back to the kitchen area.

Jed slowly ate the hot stew and sipped at the strong black coffee in a relaxed meditating silence. From the back of the room, he too watched through the front window as the townspeople went about their tasks. A familiar form rode by on a small brown and white mustang. It appeared to be Jerry Bates, a long lanky kid he had gone to school with, but he had put on weight and filled out. Still he was sure it was Jerry.

Jed finished the stew and gulped down the last of the coffee as he stood up, and leaving enough money for the bill on the table, he left to catch up with Jerry.

"Thanks. Have to go," was his quick comment as he made for the door.

He stepped through the doorway out into the road and looked back towards the church in the direction Jerry was headed. With a quick glance he noted the street was clear, but spied Jerry just walking into the Pine Mountain Saloon, his mustang tied up to the rail in front of the building.

Anxious to see his old friend he untied his own horse and walked him across and down to street to the saloon, then he retied his mount to the rail beside Jerry's horse. Going through the saloon's swinging doors he saw the short bar on the left with two tables at the far end. Across from the bar were six more vacant tables and beyond these tables along the right wall was a short hallway going by a storeroom and leading out the back door. Jed remembered there was a hitching rail at the back of the building too. Many of the ranch hands and owners that lived and worked east of town past the north end of the Black Pine Mountains came into the bar by this shorter and more convenient route.

He spotted Jerry standing near the center of the bar talking with a group of local ranch hands, his back to Jed, one foot resting on the foot rail.

Jed walked up behind him and said, "Don't believe anything Jerry tells you."

Jerry turned, mouth agape. "Jed, you old S.O.B! I heard you were home and I meant to get out to see you." He grabbed and shook Jed's hand warmly as he continued, "How the hell you doin'?" Turning to the men gathered at the bar he added, "Guys, this is my best friend, Jed Garrett, but don't believe a word he says either!" At this the entire group laughed outright as they each reached to shake his hand and welcome him to the gathering.

After a few more rough, but complimentary remarks, Jerry ordered two beers and the two old friends moved away to sit at one of the tables against the wall.

Jerry then cheerfully inquired, "How are your folks and your brother?".

"Doin' okay as near as I can see. James is just about all growed up as you know. Really they're all fine." Politely Jed then asked of his friend, "How are your folks?" remembering Molly and John Bates as devoted, hard working people. Jerry's mother Molly stood out in Jed's memory because of her beauty and charm. At one time he recalled having a crush on her and secretly wished he could find a woman of such beauty and wonder like her.

Jerry lowed his eyes and face somewhat sadly. "Not too good. 'Bout a month after you left Pa had a bad stroke. He can't move around anymore. Can't even talk. Jus' makes a low gruntin' sound. Doc Winters says there isn't anything he can do for him, so I just try to do the best I can. I put him in his chair during the day, and Ma feeds him and looks after him real good. I carry him to the outhouse, even have to hold his button down so he can pee at times. Then too, from time to time, I get one of the Christenson boys to help me with the chores and we're getting along. Jed, I'm only telling you how it is because you are my best friend." His voice dropped, "That's why I couldn't enlist and all…, I jus' kinda keep it quiet and don't say too much about it. After all, it's personal and family."

"Damn, Jerry I didn't know. I, ah.."

Jerry wanly smiled, "Hey, it will jus' delay our cattle business for awhile."

Jed knew Jerry was referring to their dreams and schemes before the war. They were both going to move to west Texas, buy a million acres of cheap land, raise cattle, ship them to Chicago and become rich business tycoons. They were going to name their ranch the 'Double J' to denote Jed and Jerry with their brand to be two J's back to back. Such were their young dreams and aspirations and it all seemed so long ago.

"I really wanted to get out to see you, but we've all had our hands full lately. Hey, let's change the subject," Jerry continued rapidly. "Let me tell you about that crazy 'ol Svenson. Shortly after you left he came here to the bar. Got all tanked up and later in the evening when he decided to go, he got up, staggered to his feet and went out the front door to get his horse. Pretty quick he was cussin' and come stormin' back in. Started screamin' he was going to 'keel da son of a bitch vit take my horse'. Naturally everyone denied taking the nag so eventually the wind went out of his sails and he slumps down in one of the chairs all dejected like."

On he went with the story, "You remember Crazy Carl who was the bartender here? He enlisted shortly after you did. Anyway Carl came out from behind the bar and put his arm around Svenson saying he'd help him find his horse. He finally got him up again on his feet and they turned and went out the back door arm in arm, and sure enough, there was his horse right out in back where it had been tied all along!"

They both began to laugh as Jerry slapped his arm on Jed's shoulder saying, "Wait, wait, that's not all! Seems like Svenson was so happy to get his horse back he insisted on giving Carl a tip!"

They both roared again as Jed added, "And I can't imagine Carl trying to discourage it either!"

Then Jerry added soberly, "You knew Carl didn't come back didn't you? Got killed in the battle at Resaca de la Palma. We all miss him. He was a good man too."

Quietly Jed replied, "No I didn't. Sorry to hear 'bout that. A Lot of good men didn't come back." Memories of other friends lost in the war flashed in his mind as he added, "Damn sad too".

Jerry took a swallow of beer and changed the subject. "Jed, there's been an awful lot of changes while you've been gone. Butcher's people have started pushing people around, off their ranches, and the like. Things around here are really heating up."

"Yes, I know. I had a run in with a couple of that bunch 'bout four weeks back. They were running their cattle in the big meadow land that Martinez and us have been sharing. You know which one I mean, the one we use for winter range."

"Know 'zactly the piece you are talkin' about," Jerry answered. "Butcher's getting too damn pushy. He's hired the Swanks brothers to do his dirty work and so far he took over the Jacobs' spread, one old place near the river and the Brown ranch north of town." He continued on, "Also Svenson's place, the Gomez land, plus another Mexican's place bordering Gomez. It was rumored that he raped one of the Gomez girls then set fire to the place."

"My God!" Jed gasped.

"That's not all. I heard from one of the hands that quit him, he's planning on wiring off all the range he can lay his hands on and we know for sure that he has rustled some of our cattle from our spread and worked over the brands too."

"But wire! Can't hardly believe a man would try to wire off the range like that. Down near Corpus Christi I heard hands talking of wire but I didn't take much stock in it. Besides, could that much wire even be available?" Jed asked. He knew his old friend might embellish a good story but he was not prone to out and out lie. Still, he had trouble believing everything.

As the two men were talking on the subject of Butcher and his crew, four of Butcher's hands came into the bar though the back door strutting in with a loud and overbearing manner. It was obvious they were not regular ranch men as they all wore weapons in holsters which were tied down. They definitely had the looks of hired gunmen.

Looking up Jerry remarked. "That is the leader of the bunch, there in the middle, the short guy with the brown hat, with the small black mustache and goatee. That's Eddie Swanks, and that's his brother Joe on the left."

"Got it."

Jed noticed that Eddie had a new Colt Walker in the holster on his hip and he wondered momentarily where he got the weapon.

Joe had the same short, wiry skeletal frame and it was easy to recognize that they were brothers. Both had round brown eyes set in small round faces, with the same short pointy noses centered therein. The quick apparent difference was that

Joe had a light, scraggly black beard that thinned out too soon as it reached up towards the bottom of his ears.

"Eddie comes to town quite often. Spends a lot of time seeing Betty Raines. She's the blond waitress across the street at Sam's."

Jed acknowledged, "Just saw her. I was over at Sam's when you went by." Jed looked across the room and added, "The guy on the far left is one of the guys I had the run-in with." Pausing, he slowly added, "I think his name is Larry if I recall rightly and the other one on the far right is the one who did all the talking. I don't know his name."

Jerry cut back in, "I don't either. Probably some drifter just hired on by Clyde."

"Look, see the table on the far left? That's reserved on Saturday nights for when Clyde Butcher comes to town. He usually arrives a little after dark. See none of those guys are sittin' there. Gives him protection from the 'riffraff' he says." Jerry continued, "You can hardly recognize Clyde. Must weigh 'bout three hundred pounds now, comes in here in his fine clothes and all, carries a small derringer tucked inside the top of his pants that you can see when the top rolls over due to the fat. I even doubt if he knows how to use the thing," with a voice of disgust Jerry continued, "...and smokes those little factory-made Mexican see-gars while he and his cronies play cards 'til closing time. Then they pour him into his buggy and head back to his place shooting off both their guns and mouths."

"Yes, I can see things sure have changed," Jed observed.

"I understand that he has been tryin' to force or buy his way into the new bank being built by the Blankenships. I swear someday, someone is going to shoot that man, of that I'm sure."

At the far table Eddie ordered a bottle of whiskey for his small entourage and taking a ten dollar bill from the large roll of money in his shirt pocket he told the new bartender they would 'drink against it'. Eddie began pouring for the rest of the men.

"Eli," he whispered quietly as he handed a drink to the man at the right. "Isn't that the man that run you and Larry out of that good low pastureland. He don't look that mean to me. Sure did make Clyde unhappy."

"Well, he had all those other guys with him then, and we didn't have any chance. They jus' came ridin' in, guns drawn and all. We just didn't have a chance," he repeated as he downed the whiskey in one swallow. He had obviously inflated the number of Garrett's men that day to save his job and his neck.

Eddie poured Eli another shot as he continued to stir and antagonize this wound in the ego of his working partner. He did not let Eli's shot glass get low either as he kept adding fuel to the fire. "There's only two of them now and that Jerry Bates isn't even packing a gun. You can take him. We're here to back you up."

"Yeah, I know I can take him." he said loud enough for Jed and Jerry to hear. "He's jus' one of those farm boys with a fancy pistol."

The comments over the loud din from Eddie's table prompted Jerry to remark, "Let's leave. That guy's pushing for a fight. I don't even have my pistol with me."

"Yeah, I agree. Let's get outta of here. I don't have any argument with any of those drunks."

Eli pressed on, "Hey Garrett, where's your army now? You're lookin' kinda yellow farmer boy!" Eddie sat there stoically with a slight fixed grin on his face.

Jed nodded in agreement at Jerry as they both rose from their table to leave. As Jed took a partial step around the table he saw Eli rise and reach to draw his pistol. Instinctively Jed's hand drew his Colt as he bent and fired in one movement.

The impact of the bullet knocked Eli backwards against the wall and he slid down the wall onto the floor, eyes wide open in shock as the noise of the shot thundered in the small building. Jed remained standing, ready to fire at anyone else who moved at Eddie's table. Blood began to seep from Eli's chest soaking his faded gray shirt. No one in the bar moved.

Eddie Swanks purposely cowered as he broke the silence. "Mr. Garrett, Let me apologize. He was out of line. Had too much to drink. I'm sorry."

At the sound of Eddie's voice pandemonium broke loose as people ran out of the front and back doors. Eddie had seen what he wanted to. Jed was good, but not fast, and Eddie knew himself to be faster. Jed bent forward every so slightly on the balls of his feet making a slightly shorter target, he made a mental note to remember that. He also knew he could have taken Jed there in the saloon, but not with four men against one in front of witnesses. No, that was not Eddie's way. He studied his opponents, determined their weaknesses, and then set the trap. Some might say he was underhanded, but it was why he was successful. The man who died mattered not. In Eddie's mind he had served his purpose.

Eddie rose slowly from the table with both of his hands grasping the lapels on the black vest he wore over a yellowish white shirt. His pose was to convey a look of non threatening. Turning and looking at the men beside him, he spoke, "Let's get outta' here." They rose obediently and rather than use the back door as was their normal custom Eddie led them towards the front entrance. As he passed Jed, he whispered in a hushed voice though clinched teeth loud enough for only

Jed to hear. "You're a dead man!" They continued out the door and crossing the street went into Sam's restaurant.

The commotion brought the curious to view the scene along with Doc Winters and Big Ed. They took one look at the dead man and knelt down beside him. Doc took his feet and Ed lifted the man under his shoulders as they packed him out of the building. "Out of the way," Doc commanded. "It's all over, nothing more to see."

At that point Hank from the Grocery and Hardware store across the street came into the building and generally took control. After talking with some of the people in the building who witnessed the shooting and knowing of the Garrett family's reputation for their integrity he asked Jed to stay in the area as they may have to send a Marshall in from Abilene or Fort Worth to review everything 'legal like'. Jed promised to stay at the ranch and to be available should the authorities want to ask further questions. Jerry and some of the others spoke up and volunteered to be available as witnesses on Jed's behalf if needed.

At last Jed mounted up to return to the ranch alone with his thoughts. What bothered him was not that he had to shoot the man, he been through that in the war, but he knew how this would affect the puritanical Christian ethics of his family. They even named both of their sons from the Bible. James and his own given name, Jedediah were Biblical. His full name was Jedediah Ames Garrett. The 'Ames' portion came from his mother's maiden name.

He knew the killing would silently gnaw at his father and cause much pain and anguish for his mother. On one hand he knew his brother James could accept the facts as they were and get on with his life. On the other hand the shooting further accentuated and magnified the earlier decision he had made to leave Wedgewood.

Further Eddie's threat did not frighten Jed. He had heard threats before. Yet for the life of him he couldn't understand why a man he had never met before threatened to kill him. The only question that concerned him about the threat was where and when the affront would occur. From what he had seen of the man he was sure he would not attack in the typical way. No, he was sure Eddie would probably look for an edge or advantage.

He broke the news as gently as he could to his family and as predicted his father sat biting his lip in stony silence while his mother left to cry in the privacy of her bedroom. Young James' only remark was terse, "He had it coming."

Word of the shooting spread rapidly through the small settlement causing a fervor of excitement and apprehension. Although there were shootings in other parts of the territory, this was the first time anyone was killed in Wedgewood.

The community as a whole agreed the man Eli, had it coming, but it still remained a stain on the moral fabric of the town and the Reverend Baker did his part to make everyone aware of it.

CHAPTER 6

▼

The following Sunday afternoon brought the long expected return of Juan and Juanita Martinez back from Austin. Even they heard the news of the shooting as they came through town which made the Garrett meeting a bit subdued. They tried to act and talk as if the killing had not happened, but all knew it was not so. It would take time for everyone to adjust.

Juan stepped from the wagon and grasped Jed's hand. "Ah Senor, you look much better now. We did not know if you would live, but you look good now I theenk."

"Yes, thanks to you and Juanita I made it. I owe you.."

"Oh, eet es nawthin' Senor," he cut in. "We are glad we can help our friends."

The men turned to task of off-loading the supplies of salt lick for the cattle, flour, cooking salt, molasses and the other sundries on the Garrett's winter shopping list after which Tom promptly paid Juan for the Garrett's share.

Jed filled Juan in on the run-in down in the big meadow with the Butcher crew while assuring him that his brother, while quite worried and shaken, was fine. He explained that they had lost only the one horse but had found and brought in some stray cattle missed in the spring roundup.

Juan stated to Tom and Edith that he and Juanita had been successful in re-filing on his property but found they were unable to complete the exact boundary descriptions that were necessary for the Garrett ranch. They did get a file number and all Tom would have to do is fill in the correct data and take the information back to Austin again before the end of November. Unfortunately that meant another trip for someone.

Juanita, even though tired from the long trip, talked with Edith about the sights she had seen in Austin and what clothes she had bought, promising to tell her more about everything later. After inquiring of Jed about his health and general condition she climbed up on the wagon and joined her father for the final leg home as she admired Jed's wavy, coal black hair. Her dark penetrating eyes took notice of his rugged handsome build with silent approval.

It had been a brief stop to leave the supplies and visit. Now they were anxious to get home so they could relax and rest.

The next two weeks bought a calm to the tense region. The fall roundup had begun for all the ranchers including Butcher as everyone had to plan for the coming winter. Jed felt sure there would be no immediate problems as the Garretts' also began their winter preparations.

Accordingly Tom, Jed, James and Cob rode with Juan and Jose as they scoured the high plateaus to the west of both ranches for their herds. The days were long and hard and being far from their ranches they camped in the open, living on jerky, beans and coffee.

The larger ranches used a traveling cook and chuck wagon similar to the brand new one that Butcher had made for his men in the field. Next year the Garretts and the Martinez families planned to pool their money and buy a used chuck wagon. Provided, of course, that they had a profitable spring sale from the cattle they presently had on hand. It was more difficult without the mobile kitchen but they would make do until they could better afford the purchase.

Therefore every third day they met Edith and Juanita at a predetermined site with a buckboard wagon load of real ranch cooking that the two women had collaborated on. The men stuffed themselves with the stews, tasty breads and pastries, determined to store up against the next two lean days of more jerky, beans and coffee.

Behind the wagon trailed extra mounts tied to a line to relieve the tired horses the men had been riding and when the women left they took the tired mounts back to the ranch to be rested.

Finally they finished the roundup of cattle on the western side of their lands and moved the herd down onto the edge of the big meadow winter pasture. With the thicker, better hay the cattle were easier to keep in check by Cob and Jose while the remaining four men rode up the southern side of the Black Pine Mountains to start the process all over again.

This was much harder territory in which to find the cattle because of the many small canyons and draws containing scrubby trees that helped hide the cattle from their pursuers and often many of the older range savvy cattle attempted to hide from the riders. The hot summer sun further added to the extreme difficulties of the roundup on this lower end of the mountains as sweat mixed with the dust and dirt of the trail got in the eyes of all as the men rode, hollered and cursed at both the cattle and the demanding conditions.

They split into pairs to flush the cattle from the hills. Tom and James would work their mounts up to the tops of the ravines and draws then painstakingly ride down through the draws forcing the cattle down to Jed and Juan to accumulate. In the afternoon they traded off as Jed and Juan would ride the top of the hills while Tom and James kept the herd intact down below. Later at the end of the day all four of the riders would push the herd back into the upper meadow to join in with the growing herd that Jose and Cob were tending.

It was late morning of the third day as Tom and James came down a gorge pushing five brown faced long horns in front of them. The dust flew from around the horses hooves as James reined up impatiently at the bottom of the draw. "By God someone's been running some of the cattle off ahead of us."

Jed answered, "How do you know?"

"'Cuz there's a lot more tracks up on top than down in the draws where the cattle normally are."

Hearing that Tom rode up alongside the two. "Let's not get hasty," he put in. "There is that possibility but those tracks are old, so we can't be sure. If it's cool some of those 'horns' will move up on top in the evening to cool off in those evening winds."

"Dad, I'm tellin' you, we're losin' some. We're just not getting as many out of these draws as we did last year," James persisted.

"Well that's true, but we may very well find a lot more in some of the draws ahead. That would explain the whole thing. Right now let's eat a bite and get a little rest before we start the afternoon push." Tom was always patient and careful to take a long look at both sides of a problem before reacting. He knew from experience that many times a quick irrational decision could case much greater problems in the long run of events.

James however, was sure that someone had rustled some of the cattle and was impatient to check it out, but calmer heads prevailed at least for the time being.

They ate their lunches in the saddle as the horses nibbled off the tops of the scant mountain summer grass. The men always alert to stragglers and strays rode slowly circling in one of the bottoms near a grove of aspen trees while containing and calming the cattle they had driven down from above. The noontime hot summer sun continued it's own quest to penetrate any few remaining patches of shade left on the hills. Both man and beast wanted refuge from it's burning rays.

Eventually Jed and Jose left the group to take their turn on the mountain slopes. Privately Jed was glad to make the afternoon push as it would give him time to look for signs of rustling too. Deliberately the two men rode up the ridge line to get at the heads of the canyons. They passed the head end of the draw that Tom and James had come down earlier and continued on to the next.

As they moved along the ridge line Jed could see some of the tracks James mentioned earlier and he silently pointed them out to Jose. Yes they were old. At least three, maybe four days at least. Might even be a week old, but he could not see any rider's horse tracks in pursuit. It was possible that his dad was right after all.

They reined up at the beginning of the coming draw and Jose moved off down the left side of the canyon. There was really nothing to be said. They didn't have to. Experience had taught each his job and how to do it. Be careful of falls, watch for stragglers, a flick of a tail, an ear, a snort, the small movement of rocks caused by a fleeing cow or calf, all captured the attention of the horse and rider who then hazed the animals down to join the others below.

Jed moved on towards the right side of the draw but before starting down he glimpsed a different track. He moved closer. It was the print of a shod horse. He continued looking in the vicinity and found a number of horse tracks. For sure, some people or someone, had ridden up here and it did appear that they were moving cattle in front. There could be explanations of course but he had seen enough evidence for now. He neck reined to his left and proceeded down the incline.

They kicked out another five head of cattle by the time they got to the bottom and after putting them in with the herd below they immediately started discussing the additional tracks Jed found up on top.

They all knew there were plausible explanations. A rancher may have been pushing his own strays back to his own ranch and may have cut though, but no one had mentioned anything to the Martinez or Garrett ranches about this as was the normal practice. Still it was a possibility. More probable, it could have been a rustler getting a few head of cattle for a seed crop for his own spread. Many a ranch got its start by rustling cattle from a neighbor. This made more sense as the number of head moved was not large. The thought arose that it could be men from the Butcher ranch to the east but this didn't set right as only about twenty head had passed through. It could be that the Indians may have stolen a few head, but this was quickly dismissed as well because Indians ponies have no horseshoes. No, they decided, it was either someone taking a few head, or someone bringing home their own strays. They could better determine that after the roundup was completely done. Their count at that time may answer the questions they voiced.

At last in early September the final roundup was over and they had amassed over 2,200 head in the big meadow pastureland. It had gone better than some past years as no one got seriously hurt. Jed got thrown twice, once by a nervous bronco and the other time when the horse he was riding stepped in a hole and both fell. Cob was knocked off of his horse by a tree limb and went head first into the ground and later Juan got cut up and scraped when the horse he was riding went loco and raced down the mountainside throwing him into a large patch of cactus. Jose got into an argument with his own lariat and while trying to untangle it, got the rope tangled around his mount's front legs and they both fell much to the amusement of the others. Only Jed's father Tom and his brother James, escaped unscathed in the roundup and thus had the bragging rights as to their horsemanship.

The weather too had cooperated. In fact it rained only twice during the entire operation and only a gentle light rain at that. There had been no sudden thunderstorms, nor tornados to frighten the cattle. Often a rock fall in the distance, a clap of thunder or any odd or unusual sound could set the cattle stampeding off across the land. It had gone well so far.

Still the task of separating the different ranches' brands and getting them to their original owners remained. This must be done before the branding of any calves that were missed in the spring roundup because only then could one determine which unbranded calf followed its branded mother to establish ownership.

Now that they were working in one place Edith and Juanita continued to coordinate on the food that each prepared at home and then brought to the men on a daily basis for their noontime meal. The meal break would usually last for about two hours as the men took their plates to eat and sit in the shade of a wagon or buggy that brought the fare.

Each man had his own style and place to hunker down while eating and resting. Jed's spot was normally at the back of either the buggy or the wagon where he could use the back of a wheel to lean against until the iron wheel rim bit into his back. Then he would slide down closer to the ground to get more comfortable. With his hat pulled down over his eyes he would then try to get some rest. Frequently Juanita would bring her plate to join him for a short time and the two would make small talk over the day's events.

Wranglers from other ranches, including Butcher's, brought Garrett and Martinez cattle back and returned to their own spreads with their respective branded cattle in tow. However, none of the hands from Butcher's spread were any of the men Jed had seen in town.

The last of the roundup came on the final day of September ending three hard, grueling weeks rounding up, herding and branding cattle. At the final count Martinez tallied 1,330 bulls, cows and calves while the Garrett share came to 1,112 animals. The final tally was high so they were unable to resolve the question whether some of the cattle might had been rustled. They may never know for sure but the suspicion lingered.

Their combined horse herd had increased by over forty head as well. It had been a very successful year and most of the owners were quite optimistic that the livestock prices would remain strong in the spring when they were to be shipped to the northeastern markets.

Often the men that returned from the war had become hard, cruel and insensitive caused by the combat they had seen and endured and in some instances this protective exterior never softened. Jed, however, did not seem to lose his sensitively and tenderness in spite of what he had been through. Perhaps it was because of the cruelty that he had seen that made him appreciate life all the more.

The final days of the endeavor had another effect as it began to draw Juanita closer to Jed. Slowly she became impressed by his strength, compassion and understanding he exhibited even after what he had seen and been through. Moreover she became fascinated and infatuated by his quiet demure, rock hard physique and self assurance. With his father's shaggy black hair, always in need of a haircut, he presented a strikingly handsome figure. Now as she turned eighteen he became the secret love of her dreams.

Jed noticed the recent impression he seemed to have made on her and his ego rather enjoyed the flirtation. He did not intentionally try to stop her nor had he encouraged her. Instead he was quite attracted to her dark flashing eyes and long black hair but he carefully sidestepped the subtle hints that Juanita now openly dropped. The roundup was over, he would be leaving soon and he did not want to become entangled and cause her any distress or discomfort in a short, tempestuous affair that could only end in heartbreak for the both of them.

At the Garrett's main ranch house there was still hay to finish cutting and bring in, hogs to butcher, the canning of fruit and the storage of food in the fruit cellar for the winter ahead.

Now that the bulk of the summer's work was over, and in spite of the past tension, those in town decided to have a dance so all could relax a little and perhaps exchange conversation while mending the fences of anxiety. The dance was to be held in a large storage building just behind Brown's Yardage store on the coming Saturday.

At last word came from Doc Winters and Hank Nelson that there was to be no charges entered against Jed for the shooting as it was in self defense as seven witnesses had already testified. But that did not erase the concern that Jed felt. He heard through Cob that some of the women were complaining in Sam's Restaurant about a killer living in the area. Knowing he was the reason for the town's apprehension Jed decided not to attend the dance.

It was finally Cob who helped him understand that the town would be forced to confront the problem and that meant Jed must be seen. What had happened, happened and could not be changed. People whose touchy morals were fractured would have to look him in the face. If he didn't put in an appearance, things would still be swept under the carpet and the healing process for the town would take much longer.

There were some in town who voiced concern that Butcher and his crowd might somehow ruin the entire proceedings that were planned for the occasion. Therefore six of the local men, including Jerry Bates, offered to give their time to act as roving pickets for the evening. It was felt that the pickets would act as a determent to any possible violence. With the precautions in place enthusiasm began to heighten.

As they rode towards town Jed began to brighten and look forward to the dance. Tom and Edith were riding in the buggy while Cob and Jed lagged casually behind. Because of the unrest in the air James was elected to remain at the ranch and keep an eye on things. Tom and Edith had already decided to leave the dance early and come back to the ranch to let the anxious and impatient young man put in an appearance later in the evening.

As they rode past the church it was readily apparent that there was a big turnout. The area in front of the businesses were choked with wagons, buggies and horses all tied to the hitching rails leaving no more room so they made their way around behind Brown's yardage store before finally tying up at the back of the building.

The music and dancing had already begun as they entered the already crowded building, the wooden floor moving up and down to the foot beat of the dancers. The band was in the back left corner of the building and the makeshift band was playing with zestful enthusiasm. Two banjos, one guitar and one fiddle rounded out the loud ensemble.

Just inside the entrance the men were asked to lay any firearms on the table provided and both Jed and Cob complied with the request. They were also reminded that whiskey was not allowed at the dance, but all knew that outside the building many of the men had a bottle stashed in their buggies or in a saddle-bag. It only proved that men who want can always find a way to get a drink of the spirits.

As Jed squeezed into the full building he looked about for familiar faces. He was pleasantly surprised to have many men step forward to warmly shake his hand and welcome him to the dance while he slowly made his way around the room. It looked as if the healing process may have started.

When the music and dance stopped for a moment Hank Nelson asked for quiet and welcomed everyone, thanking them all for coming, and like the savvy storekeeper he was, discreetly complimented the ladies on their finery and the work they had put forth for the decorations and the food.

As Jed looked about the room he could see his father talking with Juan Martinez and another man. Due to his height Tom was easy to see in the crowd. Jed spotted Jerry Bates standing near the doorway and nodded an acknowledgment and made eye contact from across the room.

The music started again, this time in a slower beat as 'ladies' choice' was announced by the band. It was the opening Juanita had been waiting for. She had been watching the door wishing for Jed to attend the party and was thrilled to see him at last. Making her way to him she boldly took hold of his arm. Pulling him out onto the dance floor she coyly pleaded, "Dance with me please, please."

Jed willingly followed her onto the floor saying, "I didn't know you knew how to dance."

"There's a lot of things you don't know about me," she teased back as she snuggled into his strong arms. "I know what I like and I know what I don't like," she added. In a sexy pout she continued, "I like most of the things about you."

He continued the flirtation, "You mean there's something you don't like?"

The evening wore on with most of Jed's time being occupied by Juanita. Only twice did she give him room to dance with any of the other ladies in the room and she did so only with an eye to learn from her competition how to enhance her next dance with him.

When Jed was not being monopolized by Juanita he noted Eddie Swanks was present and dancing with Betty Raines, the strawberry blond waitress from Sam's Restaurant. By now Jed was sure that anything that was said around Betty made its way right back to Eddie. Even so Eddie was abiding by the rules and that was a good sign, the pickets evidently were having the desired effect. Before long his father and mother waved their early farewells to all as they left as planned to relieve a frustrated James still at home. Cob too had found a cute young lady and was whirling around the floor as if he understood what he was doing.

The dance seemed to be having the desired effect intended. So far the only ripple in the water had been a remark by the newcomer to town, Mrs. Betty Blankenship who asked rather arrogantly, "Why are Mexicans here?" She was abruptly put her place by Clara Dixon who curtly replied, "Because they live here, that's why."

As the music played Juanita continued to keep Jed to herself. He found he was enjoying the smell and warmth of her supple body, her breasts burning into his body, exciting him. During a break in the music they walked outside the building into the starry night hand in hand. Wordlessly and away from the music's din they walked. They lingered in the shadows of a moonlit building where they kissed passionately and embraced.

Suddenly she pulled away from him, "I have to get back to the dance," she gasped breathlessly. "My father will wonder where we are. I have to go," adding in a soft whisper, "Meet me tomorrow at Flat Creek. I'll bring a box lunch." With that she left his arms, turning and running back into the building.

Jed stood there in the dark bewildered and confused, yet excited by her advance and wondering just where to go and what to do now. He finally decided the best thing would be to pick up his sidearm and ride back to the ranch and think things over.

He wrestled with his dilemma during the night, but in the end his desire to see Juanita again won out. And as he rode to the rendezvous he could see from a distance that she was waiting at the creek as promised. Her horse was tied off downstream next to a stand of small cottonwoods. Higher on the bank behind her a woven lattice lunch basket sat on a multicolored Mexican blanket.

Juanita looked beautiful wearing a white peasant blouse with the edge pulled down over one shoulder in a provocative manner. The blouse had brown trimming matching the delicate brown of the full skirt she wore. She was sitting on the edge of the blanket with her bare feet in the slow moving water. She looked radiant as the sun shone on her shoulder length long black hair. Her satiny smooth skin and her sparkling black eyes were mesmerizing, her bright lips tempting and alluring.

As he rode up she spoke, "I didn't know if you were coming."

"I almost didn't."

"Why did you?"

"I don't know, I just had to see you again."

"I'm glad you came." She patted the blanket and added, "Come on, sit down and eat."

Juanita opened the basket containing a assortment of still warm bread, freshly grown ripe tomatoes, pickles, hot peppers, two apples, butter, jelly, hot sauce and a large piece of ham and another of beef. She even included a partial bottle of homemade red wine she had taken from her Uncle Jose's stash.

"I can't believe all the food you brought!" he exclaimed in surprise. "You came prepared to feed a small army."

"Come help yourself, let's eat." was her quiet reply.

They ate slowly, immersed in their own thoughts as they picked through the array spread before them. After the leisurely buffet Juanita gathered up the plates and utensils they had used and washed them in the stream before putting them back into the basket along with the remaining food.

While she was cleaning up Jed took the time to pour them each a glass of the deep red wine, silently handing one of the glasses to her. They sat side by side basking in the beauty of the day, the world, and each other. She appeared luscious in the brilliant sunshine as he noted her ample breasts were covered only by her blouse.

His hands moved slowly to her arms, his fingers lightly moving up and down her smooth skin. She finished the wine, setting the glass aside, and nestled into his arms as he wrapped them around her. He bent and kissed her full moist lips, long, hard and passionately, their bodies pressing together in anticipation.

His hands moved under her blouse, his fingers warm to her skin, cupping her firm, young succulent breasts. She lay back on the blanket surrendering to his advances. Faster now his hands moved under her skirt to explore. He found the mound of love that she eagerly pushed hard against his hand.

Crazed with lust of the moment at hand he undid his belt and sliding down his pants he moved on top, his throbbing, rigid passion penetrating her body as she groaned in complete ecstasy. Together they luxuriated in the glow of one another. Their desires were complete in the act of love.

They lay by the stream the rest of the afternoon, he content with the world, and she patiently and tenderly kissing his neck, arms and chest. When she at last lay still in his arms she faintly hummed a tune in the joy of their shared experience.

As day began to ebb they stirred from their nest by the water's edge and nibbled on the food still left in the basket. They lingered on with soft touches and warm, gentle kisses.

Reluctantly they packed up what was left of the food and rolled up the blanket. He turned and walked downstream bringing back her horse. Then he stowed the picnics items in the saddlebags.

Juanita quietly said, "I must go now. When will I see you again?"

Unsure of himself he replied, "Soon, I can't say just now, but I'll work it out. We've hayin' to finish, but I'll work it out."

She whispered, "I love you."

They stood together above the stream, she on her toes, kissing fervently in a long, close embrace before they separated. The sun was lowering on the horizon casting their shadows out behind them. They both knew it would never be the same for either of them.

During the rest of the summer Jed worked alongside the other men as they swung the scythes cutting the tall wild hay in and around the big meadow. Day by day they cut, raked, and loaded the hay onto the wagons pitchfork by pitchfork. Their only rest came as they rode the full wagon loads back to the barns only to pitch the load bit by bit into a seemingly endless hay loft. It was hard, backbreaking work with sweat running down their backs and aching muscles crying out for relief from morning until evening.

They planned to fill the Garrett barn first then finish with the Martinez barn. Jed did not know which was harder, a roundup with long, hard hours in the saddle, or the slow meticulous gathering of the hay. Both made the men silently wish for the slow times of a cooling winter snow. They retired early and slept unmoving until rousted in the mornings.

Even after a long, wearisome day Jed had trouble sleeping. He began to take evening walks down the road and past the barn following the corral fence for about two hundred feet where the fence turned at a small stand of junipers and went westward. On past the trees he walked alone and troubled with his thoughts.

He felt both confused and guilty. This was not what he planned. The time was approaching for him to leave as he had to fly free from the still strained family atmosphere. Only the rover Cob, sensed the problems he was having but was unable to break into Jed's troubled world.

He had delayed telling his mother and father of his decision. It appeared to him that everyone including his own family and the rest of the town must have time for the memories of the killing to diminish. That meant he would have to leave for a while. And what of Juanita? He felt guilty for taking advantage of a beautiful, young, impressionable and trusting woman. She was too young. He felt four years was too wide a chasm. Did he love her? Of course he felt a love for her but was it deep enough he asked himself. And where would they go? What could he do? It was a different relationship than that of the fast women he had known in Mexico. In those affairs there were no ties to bind and torture later. During the day and night he mentally wrestled with these problems.

CHAPTER 7

▼

To aid with the family finances Jerry Bates' mother Molly had occasionally worked at Sam's Restaurant in town as most of the men were aware. The men would make excuses to drop by to have coffee and flirt with her but she easily kept them in their place with her quick tongue, humor and wit. Over time many of the local teenage men had their first crushes on the comely woman, and at one time even Jed Garrett.

Molly had been rather plain of appearance as a poor young girl growing up in west Tennessee. It could be said she was a late bloomer and as she aged her beauty seemed to blossom from her pleasant demeanor. She was quietly precocious, yet at the same time still outgoing.

The entire family worked long hours planting, hoeing and picking crops on the dirt farm her father had cleared from the wooded hillsides. Later at the age of thirteen she talked herself into a cleaning job in the local hardware store. She became very dependable and the owner began to allow her to help out behind the counter with the customers. As a result her self-confidence improved and as the time went by she became a very personable, engaging young woman.

She was always groomed and dressed meticulously, her blond hair worn long, but not quite down to her shoulders. Her blue eyes fairly sparkled with enthusiasm when she spoke and her gaiety was contagious to those around her while her svelte and lithe body soon became the envy of her sisters.

The men in the area began to take notice of the striking young woman and vie for her attention. With a smile and a quick or witty word, she courteously spurned all offers except from the quiet John Bates. The day she saw him she decided he was the man for her. They dated for almost a year before John got up the nerve to ask her to marry him.

Soon after they married Jerry was born. Times were hard but John was a diligent worker, sometimes working two jobs to make ends meet. It was a very close relationship and she was completely devoted to her husband and young son. They tried to have more children over the years without success but it did not discourage either of them and they graciously accepted the fact that it was not to be.

They were happy and content with their lives. In the early years of their marriage they scrimped and saved their modest earnings and when they heard stories that rich farm land in Texas could be bought very reasonably they took the plunge and came further west settling north of Wedgewood on some of the less fertile land that they were able to afford.

John spent his time over the succeeding years painstakingly building up a small herd of some fifty cattle. He cleared the nearby fields of rocks and scrub trees, irrigated and planted hay, oats and barley to supplement the scant wild grasses that grew in his area.

Molly realized over time that her beauty had become an asset. She did not flaunt it, rather she took silent pride in that fact and always tried to look her best. However, no one could tempt her to stray from John's side. He was, and would always remain, the man of her life.

After John's stroke she remained at home with him. Jerry now worked the fields and tended to the animals and she did her best to assist her disabled husband. Every day, sometimes with Jerry's help, she lovingly washed him, dressed and combed his hair. After hand-feeding him she would take the pillows and prop him up in his chair so he could look out the window. This she did cheerfully while quietly singing and talking to the mute form in his paralyzed shell. Doc Winters frequently came by and tried to administer every possible medical aid he could think of. Nothing seemed to help.

Yet John knew and understood everything though he was unable to move or talk. He could blink his eyes and they developed a way of communicating. Three blinks for yes, two for no. Even in this form their love for one another remained unshakable as they often sat side by side, her hand reaching out to comfort and hold his.

Late Thursday afternoon Eddie Swanks rode north as he was directed to do by Clyde Butcher. He proceeded along the dusty path leading to the Bates property and reined up at the rail in front of the small unassuming cabin located below

Mason Hill. Walking up to the cabin door he knocked and Molly Bates opened the door.

With one hand holding the small lapel on the black vest he wore he asked to see Jerry. Molly explained he was out cutting hay with the Christenson boy and they would not be in until dark or thereabouts. Eddie than gave her a message for Jerry which gave her cause to wonder. Cunningly polite he touched the brim of his hat, gave a slight bow of acknowledgment, and stepped down from the porch, remounted and rode back down the trail.

Over a late supper Jerry and his mother discussed the message that Eddie had left earlier that day. It sounded like Clyde Butcher had a business offer of some kind for Jerry and asked him to meet him the following day at Sam's Restaurant around noon. He might be late, but not to worry, he would meet him there.

They had no idea what Clyde had in mind. Perhaps it was to buy them out or try to hire Jerry. It was all quite puzzling and they discussed it at great length always speaking in loud enough tones so John could hear the entire conversation.

They discussed the possibilities. If it were to buy them out Jerry could listen to the offer and they could think it over, but again Clyde never paid a fair price for any property that they were aware of. Undoubtedly he knew that John was unable to work the ranch any longer and that they might need the money. Yes, they could definitely use the money that was true. If not that, what possible business venture could it be? And as for hiring on, Jerry was adamant and said, "he'd never work for the man."

They debated most of the evening and finally decided that Jerry would go to town and at least meet with Clyde. He'd then come home and they would discuss whatever it was together. Since John had been listening to the late evening dialogue they asked him if he agreed with them. He blinked his eyes three times as an answer.

The next day Jerry left the cabin around ten in the morning so as to arrive at Sam's near noon. As he rode along he wondered if perchance he might see his friend Jed. Probably not as he reasoned the Garretts were still putting in hay for winter.

Nearing town he noted that the streets were relative free of people. "Tomorrow being Saturday, things would be a lot busier," he mused. Only two wagons were tied up at Hank's Hardware and Grocery. On the other side of the street, just north of The Pine Mountain Saloon, the carpenters were busy putting siding up on new bank building.

Butcher's buggy was not in front of Sam's when he pulled up and tied his mount up to the rail, comfortable knowing that he would be on time for their meeting. No one was inside as he entered the building so he took one of the tables in front of the window so he could watch the street.

"Just bring me coffee, and as a second thought, maybe a piece of pie or cake if you've got it," he said to Betty Raines when she approached his table. It was the same blond he had seen dancing with Eddie Swanks last Saturday night at the dance.

"Got apple pie, but we don't fix cakes here."

"Sounds good, then that's what I'll have."

As he methodically ate the pie he glanced out the window awaiting the arrival of Clyde Butcher. He dug out the old silver-cased pocket watch that had belonged to his dad and noticed that it read eleven fifty-five. Well, he could wait for a while he decided.

He finished the pie and sipped away at the coffee patiently waiting. Twelve-thirty came and went. No sign of Clyde. When the waitress came over to fill his coffee cup again he inquired, "Say, you haven't received any message from Butcher for me?"

"No, not a thing Jerry."

"Thanks," and then he thought, I wonder how she knows my name? Probably from her boyfriend Eddie Swanks.

Another half hour passed with no sign of his man. He got up and paid the twenty cents he owed for the pie and coffee including the fresh cup he brought back to the table.

"Damn him!" he thought for making him wait. Then giving the 'Devil his due,' he remembered that Eddie Swanks had told his mother that he might be late. "Another half hour!" he thought impatiently. One-thirty came and went. Jerry sat at the window silently seething.

When two o'clock came he stormed out of the restaurant telling the waitress that if Butcher came in, tell him he could, "Go to hell!" Still mad as he could be he mounted his horse and turned towards home. "Wasted a whole damn day for nothin'!"

It took a lot to upset Jerry and during the long ride back home he continued to be infuriated at himself for even considering meeting with Butcher. It had always been difficult to get Jerry mad but once fired up he would fight nonstop in spite of the odds against him. By his late teens he learned to keep his temper somewhat in check. Finally, he was beginning to cool off by the time he arrived back at the cabin.

He rode past the front of the small building taking notice only that the front door was partially open and proceeded around back to the barn. After unsaddling and putting his mount out to pasture he returned to the cabin using the front porch entrance.

He walked through the open door, instantly shocked to see his father lying face down on the floor and his chair lying on its side. "Hey, Mother what's,…" he started to say more but instead reached out with one hand and sat the chair upright. Then bending down he turned his father over, picked up his fragile frame, and placed him carefully back in the chair.

His father opened his eyes and grunted as loud as he could while rapidly blinking his eyes. In his bewildered state Jerry did not notice.

"Mother where in the world are you?" he hollered taking a step towards the open door to the bedroom on his right. He stopped abruptly, stunned as he saw her lifeless form on the bed. She appeared to have been horribly assaulted and mutilated. The scene was too much to take in and he sank to his knees on the floor.

"Oh my God no! No, no.." He repeated, "Oh God no!" He sat shaken at the horrible sight before his eyes then crawled to the bed and started to sob aloud.

His mother lay naked across the bed, her head turned slightly, blood still dripping from the large visible hole near the top of her head. There were deep knife cuts on her face, neck and body, the kind made to intentionally make one bleed and suffer. Both breasts were sadistically cut by teeth marks and scarred by burns. Pubic hair had been burned and some of it brutally torn from her body. Her legs hanging over the edge of the bed, cut and scratched, bore telltale marks of having been tied down while she was being raped. The clothes she had been wearing lay torn, bloody and scattered in the bed and on the floor. All signs presented the unthinkable signature of a demented, psychotic predator.

Jerry continued to cry. Tears came flooding from his eyes and down his face. He could not move, he could not think. It was a picture straight from the depths of hell.

How long he sat there in anguished shock he did not know but eventually he moved as something told him to wash and clean her ravaged body. "No one is to see her like this, no one!" he vowed silently.

He moved in a stupor as he went to the kitchen, lit the wood cooking stove and put water to boil in a large metal tub, remaining by the stove unmoving and unthinking until the water warmed. He put some of the water in a smaller pail along with soap and wash cloths and began the cleansing.

Tearfully he lightly washed away blood and cleaned over the burns. Crying and moaning he completed the job then tenderly wrapped her in a fresh sheet before laying her on the floor. Next he gathered up the blood covered sheets, blankets and clothing from the bed and floor then using a scrub brush along with strong lye soap he worked at removing the blood stains which had penetrated the mattress. As nightfall came he lit the kerosene lantern and continued working into the darkness. After picking up a throw rug and the old rifle beside the bed he scoured the wooden floor on his hands and knees. He never felt the slivers that came from the floor and ripped into his fingers.

Jerry never knew his mother had survived the attack or that his father had tried to come to her aid when he heard her screams of agony. After her attacker left she finally managed to untie herself. She knew instinctively that she had been disfigured for life. She knew also without question that she could never look at anyone again without feeling the shame inflicted on her body nor could she bear to face her son or anyone else and live again with pride. As she saw John on the floor, apparently dead, she knew her torture would last forever. There was no reason to continue on. She took down the loaded hunting rifle from the bedroom wall and placed the muzzle in her mouth. She pushed the trigger with her toe.

Jerry took the blood soaked bedding and clothing outside to be burned. He spent the rest of the night working by lantern light in the barn building her coffin. He worked all night long and with the morning light he dug her grave at 'her quiet spot' behind the cabin and barn near the base of Mason Hill. Later in the morning after he had laid her to rest he burned the bedding and the rest of the clothing.

He became totally unfeeling, still numbed by the shock of it all. His father remained in his chair from the night before and as Jerry passed back and forth during the night he continued to try to speak. Only a grunting sound came forth.

Jerry entered the house and inspected the bedroom again only then did he hear his father's cry. He leaned close to his mouth hearing only "Er, er." Over and over he repeated the sound. "Er, er." At last through his stupor, Jerry was able to comprehend his meaning.

"Was it Butcher?"

His father blinked three times. Jerry reached out and touched his father reassuringly on his shoulder then found the old rifle again, wiped the blood off the muzzle and reloaded, before walking wordlessly out of the house.

CHAPTER 8

▼

Jed still had not told his parents of the decision he made about leaving, nor had he met again with Juanita even though she had sent along a note with Jose on Thursday asking when she might see him again. His conscience continued to be tormented with anguish and apprehension.

Sometime next week after the Garrett barn was full they would start taking in the hay for Juan and he would see her then. He must tell her before then. Perhaps this weekend he might go to see her and explain why he had to move on. He only hoped he could make her understand.

He walked down the lane past the barn as he had been doing each evening as he tried to work out of his dilemma. He heard a noise near the barn. Probably one of the horses, or maybe it was Cob returning from the outhouse before turning in for the evening. The sound seemed nothing to be concerned about. Then he noted that it was starting to get dark earlier. As he walked he again thought about and worried about his situation with Juanita.

There would always be someone to point out that he had killed one of their own. Right or wrong it would be remembered. And some brash young gunslinger would eventually come to seek him out and try to make a name for himself in a gunfight. Nor would it end. It could only cause further crises as James would be forced to defend Jed's action while his parents would have to contend with the unspoken silence of the subject among their friends and neighbors. It could actually become a wedge between families. And Juanita was too young for him; he had shamefully taken advantage of the vulnerability of her youth. Further people tend to be critical of a Mexican girl and a Caucasian together. Yes he loved her, but it was too soon. It was all so overwhelming. He had to find his, or perhaps their destiny.

He walked past the empty end of the corral alone in his thoughts when he was startled to hear a horse snort. Looking up he saw a black mare tied behind the corner stand of small junipers. It was saddled up all ready to go but he could see no one around. Cautiously he walked up to the animal and looked it over carefully. It moved nervously as he walked around the animal trailing one hand on the horse's back.

To calm the animal he said quietly, "Hey, what are you doing here?"

Then he saw a 'B' the left rear hip of the horse! "Butcher! What the hell is going on?" He looked around in the evening darkness trying to locate the rider. With the horse tied to the bushes the rider had to be close by. Jed moved back under the cover of the trees to wait for his return, then he'd damn sure get some answers!

It went "Whoosh" like a blast of air being suctioned up in a draft!

Jed turned and looked through the juniper branches in the direction of the barn. "Fire! Oh my God it's a fire!" his brained screamed.

At the same moment a person was running from the barn in his direction. In the background he heard Cob shout from the bunkhouse, "Fire, fire!"

The runner dashed to the corner of the corral and vaulted over the fence. When the man turned the corner to mount up Jed grabbed his shirt with his left hand and hit him squarely in the face with his right fist.

"You son of bitch!" he yelled. He picked him up from the ground and could see his face in the light of the flames from the barn. It was Joe Swanks. He hit him again.

"No, please no!" Joe cried out.

"Why you bastard, why?"

"It was Clyde's idea. It was Clyde's idea. Don't hit me," he pleaded.

"Why.., why?" Jed repeated as he hit him another time.

Blood and a tooth came from his mouth as Joe coughed, "Please don't..."

Jed gripped Joe's shirt lifting him up to hit again.

"Clyde told me to, please..," he begged.

As Jed held the quivering form he yelled, "Who took the money from the saddle bags?" Jed had no idea why he asked this question, it just came tumbling out.

Too confused to think the scared figure replied, "It was Eddie, I didn't do it."

Jed suddenly realized it all made sense now.

"Who shot the rider?"

"It was Eli. Honest, it was Eli," he repeated cowering backwards. "Eddie said he was a better shot with a rifle, honest to God it was Eli!"

"Why?" Jed asked again.

"Butcher knew old man Garrett was going to Austin to re-file on his land and he sent us to get the legal property writin' away from him so he could file on the property as his own." A look of shock and terror spread instantly on Joe's face when he realized what he had just said.

Jed let the beaten and dazed man drop to the ground and looked toward the burning barn.

Joe sat in a heap, sobbing and gasping for breath through a broken nose and tears mixing into the blood on his face. His mind racing, he knew he could tell of Butcher's part and not worry. He and his brother could always move on to work for someone else, but now he had implicated Eddie. Eddie would kill him for this. He had to make it right. He reached for his gun.

Out of the corner of his eye Jed saw Joe reach for his gun. Jed drew his own Colt and fired. The bullet struck Joe squarely in his chest knocking him backwards to the ground. He was dead when he hit the dirt.

The noise of the shot was deadened by the roaring flames coming from the barn. Jed turned and ran to the barn to help. Edith and Cob were carrying buckets of water from the well behind the house and throwing the water on the flames. Tom was busy pulling harnesses, halters, tools and anything else he could save from the fire's path. James was trying to pull the two wagons away from the side of the barn where they had been left earlier in the day.

The livestock in the west corner of the corral were pushing against the wooden fence. The cattle were mooing with fright while the horses were pushing one another and snorting in fear, the younger mustangs rearing up and whinnying in panic.

As Jed approached he yelled, "Cob, Did you get your things out of the bunkhouse?"

"Yeh, I got most of it."

Jed joined the others as they threw more buckets of water on the fire. Finally they could see the effort was futile so they stood back from the heat to watch and try to contain the blaze as much as possible. The walls of the barn blackened, bent inward, and collapsed in on themselves as the flames shot high into the night sky. Sparks from the collapsed barn flew through the smoky clouds and landed on the roof of the house. James quickly climbed up onto the roof and put out the small starter fires.

Into the night the fire continued burning, the densely packed hay acting as a continual source of fuel for the flame's unsatiable appetite. All night long they put out smaller fires and watched as the fire eventually ebbed in the early dawn.

They assessed the situation that remained. They had saved all the livestock, most of the saddles, harnesses and reins, horse collars, singletrees, doubletrees, pitchforks and other tools from the barn. Most important they had saved the main house.

At last they stumbled wearily into the house to rest. Edith heated up the coffee and made the men a quick meager breakfast of bacon and eggs and after washing off most of the soot and ash they sat down to eat and discuss what happened.

Cob started, "I was jus' coming back from the outhouse when I heard a noise in the barn. I didn't really think much of it and went on into the bunkhouse but then from inside the room I could hear the horses raising all sorts of hell. That's when I went back out and saw the fire. Right away I opened the doors and the horses came flying out then I started hollering 'fire'."

Tom turned towards Jed, "Didn't I hear a shot?"

"Yeah it was Joe Swanks. I was walking down by the corner of the corral and saw him running out of the barn trying to get away. He pulled the gun on me and I had no choice. Guess he's still laying there." Jed did not mention what else he had learned from the dead man.

Tom took command of the situation. "This has gone on long enough and it's time it stopped!" Turning to Cob he ordered, "You load Swanks in the wagon and take him back to Butcher. He doesn't have any ax to grind with you so you should be okay. On the way back stop at every ranch you can and tell them we are having a meeting here tomorrow morning. Tell them to skip church and be here! It's time for the rest of us to band together and run that Butcher bunch out of Texas forever!"

Cob nodded in agreement and rose from the table while swallowing the last of his coffee saying, "I'll do it."

As he went out the door Jed spoke, "Wait, I'll come and give you a hand."

The two men picked through the fire-scorched harnesses finally picking out a good set along with a horse collar and halter and outfitted Blackie. Cob grabbed a singletree which they connected up the wagon then they both stepped up into the wagon and rode past the still smoldering remains of the barn to the corner of the corral.

The dead man lay where he had fallen and they loaded him into the wagon. As Cob threw a horse blanket over the figure Jed untied the black mare which was still tied to the juniper trees and tied her behind the wagon. "Give the horse back too," he said, and then putting his arm on Cob's shoulder added, "Tell Eddie Swanks that I'll meet him this evening at the Pine Mountain Saloon." Jed too had a score to settle.

The family spent the rest of the morning picking up and sorting through the debris. Other than what they had already saved nothing more could be salvaged. Finally they went back into the house to get some much needed rest, all but Jed who said he was going to take a ride to relax and clear his mind. He took a saddle and bridle off the fence, saddled Maggie and rode off in the direction of Wedgewood.

He still didn't know why he had asked Joe who took the money, then he recalled seeing a roll of cash come out of Eddie Swanks pocket when he and Jerry were in the saloon. It had to be his subconscious mind working. "It all makes sense now," he thought to himself.

Butcher and his crew had heard from someone that Tom Garrett was going to go to Austin to re-file on his land. After all it was a small town and there are no secrets in a small town. Everyone knew what everybody else was doing, but they did not know Tom had changed his mind at the last moment and had given the information to Juan to use and file for him. "How ironic," Jed reasoned, "The property description was not complete anyway and would have been of no use to them."

By happenstance he had ridden by at the very time they were setting up to ambush his father. His father being taller, perhaps might have taken the fatal bullet to his head, and if someone were killed way out in the desert no one would suspect anyone from Wedgewood. It had been a good devious plan. After taking the horse they would naturally go through the saddlebags. That's when Eddie found the money in with the rest of Jed's personal items. It would be too much of a risk to keep the horse, so he sold it to someone passing through. "I wonder where the saddle and the saddlebags went," he puzzled. "Probably sold them at the same time."

When the trio heard later that Doc Winters had a patient who had survived numerous wounds Eddie correctly assumed, with the help of some mail he had seen in Jed's saddlebags, that he was Tom Garrett's son. That's why Eddie threatened him in the bar. He was perceived to be another obstacle to overcome before they could take over the Garrett ranch. Jerry Bates mentioned something too in the saloon about Butcher setting fire to one of the other ranches to scare out the owners. It all fit together nicely.

He totaled up his losses. "Let's see, he owes me for one horse, saddle, saddle bags, a rifle, my money and for the attempt on my father's life which turned out to be an attack on me instead, and that doesn't even count Joe burning down the barn with all the hay in it."

It was still early afternoon when Jed got to Wedgewood but it was the exact time he wanted to arrive. Looking up and down the street he decided that everything had the appearance of a normal busy late afternoon in a small town. It would be quite a while yet before the Saturday night rowdy bunch turned up at the Pine Mountain Saloon.

Jed rode up to the saloon, tied Maggie to the rail in front, and walked inside. Three ranch hands were standing at the bar drinking beer and having a quiet discussion. They hardly looked up as he came in and walked past the front window to a table in the front right-hand corner of the building and sat down. He raised his arm to acknowledge the bartender and ordered a glass of beer.

He picked the table in the corner so he would be able to see Eddie come in the back door, or if by some wild chance Eddie should come through the front door then he would have a clear view in that direction as well. Jed made a point to be there before Eddie would arrive. Further he was determined to take no unnecessary chances with the man he had challenged.

Jed knew that neither his dad nor James had any experience against a gunfighter. Because of the attempt on his life and his father's life by Eddie Swanks, Jed knew he was the only one that would stand a chance against the man. The others were all ranchers without gun fighting experience. Many others may die if Butcher's cutthroats were not stopped.

He sipped at the warm beer and thought, I've got position on him. With my back to the corner no matter what he does, I'll have the best spot from which to react. He really didn't expect Eddie until early evening but he made up his mind to see his quarry before he was seen.

After being up all night fighting the fire Jed was dead tired and was not mentally as alert as he hoped to be. Perhaps fully rested he may have asked, "Would Eddie Swanks tried to outflank him? Would he send his men out to surround him? Would he purposely not come? Or would he just wait and hope that Jed would drink too much alcohol and become an easier target?" However his tired mind made none of these assessments.

He sat at the table as the heat of the day seeped into his tired body. While he waited he tried to be silently alert to any sound. His mind wandered back to his mentor Ben McCulloch in the Texas Rangers who had told them very succinctly, "Plans change in the heat of battle." That was true he knew, but not too much can change from a simple plan. It was meant be straightforward, or least that is how he had intended it to be.

*   *   *   *

Cob made the long ride to the Butchers' and Eddie Swanks was livid when he saw his brother's body in the wagon but he remained in quiet control of himself. He had learned long ago not to let his emotions get the best of him. Eddie remained mute too when Cob relayed the message that Jed wanted to meet him at the Pine Mountain Saloon tonight.

Larry, Eli's former companion, took Joe's body and laid it carefully near the barn. He then untied the black mare from the back of the wagon and led her to the corral as Cob turned his wagon around and left.

Eddie suddenly realized this was the opportunity that he had been looking for! He was about to put one more obstruction behind him.

He turned and walked over to Larry saying, "Saddle up one of those fresh horses in the corral and take a ride into town. Keep an eye out for Jed Garrett. Jus' tell me later if you see him and where he is. Don't bother him! I'll be following right behind you in about an hour. Look for me in Sam's."

Eddie waited and watched as Larry mounted up and rode off on a bay mare with a white blaze on its head, only then did he turn and go to the house. Walking in the door he saw Clyde dressed in his dark blue velour robe sitting in an large overstuffed chair while holding cold compresses to his forehead.

"What the hell's going on out there?" Clyde asked through blurry eyes.

"Joe's dead. One of Garrett's men brought back the body. Said Jed Garrett caught 'im settin' the fire…, but don't get excited. I've figured out how to get rid of the son of a bitch."

Clyde exploded up out of his chair and screamed as he threw a towel on the floor, "By God you'd better! I need that pastureland for the extra cattle that are coming in."

Eddie knew he was referring to the men he had hired to skim off small herds of twenty or so at a time from the larger surrounding ranches. In almost all cases no one even noticed the losses and they were quickly branded with the Butcher 'B' brand and put in with Butcher's main herd. If there was a original brand that could not be blotted out by using a thicker than normal 'B', that animal was butchered for local ranch use or sold off to unsuspecting buyers. The crews quickly learned that the Garrett 'G' could be made into the Butcher 'B' quite easily. Oh, a few of the ranchers suspected what was going on, but so far no one could prove it.

Clyde found that about twenty-five such forays resulted in a growth of more than six hundred additional free head of cattle to his herd. Later every head would be worth twenty dollars each as long as the northern market continued to hold. This contributed to his own philosophy, "Just take a little from everyone. They'll not even notice and you'll end up bigger than all the others."

He continued yelling at Eddie and pacing the floor, "If you can't get the job done I'll sure as hell find someone who can!"

"Don't worry 'bout it!" Eddie barked back. "Jed will be dead today, then we'll run off the rest of those damn Garretts. I'm heading to town now to take care of it."

"By God you'd better be! I've had enough of this God damn bullshit! Now get the hell outta' here. Get it done right this time and let me rest!" Clyde dropped back into his chair and reached into the bucket for another cold towel to put on his forehead adding, "I'll be coming in later, and this time you damn well better be right!"

Eddie slammed the door behind him as he stormed out of the house. He had noticed that Clyde's headaches were becoming more frequent and severe making it difficult to reason with the man. He knew too, that in spite of the headache, Clyde would eventually get up and come into town to make sure he did his job, plus he never missed his Saturday night card game with his cronies.

*   *   *   *

As Jerry Bates rode towards the Butcher ranch part of the numbness in his mind began to clear. Somewhat rational thought began to permeate as he formatted his vengeance. The north side of the Black Pine Mountains were more heavily covered with scrub pine than the rest of the hills further south and there were more hills that the road wound through as well. He picked a rock outcropping beside the road and tying his horse out of sight found a concealed spot above the road and sat back to wait. Clyde would eventually ride by, he was sure.

A rider in an empty wagon soon came by pulled by one horse. Jerry wasn't sure, but the man resembled one of Garrett's ranch hands. Shortly a lone rider came by. It was one of Butcher's hired hands and he let him pass. An hour later Eddie Swanks rode by as Jerry thought to himself, "I'll see you later in town." None of the riders had an any idea they were being watched as they rode by.

Jerry Bates continued his long watch beside the road. He turned, stretching his legs out to get more comfortable as he leaned back against the rocks behind him. He was determined to remain as long as it took. It didn't make any difference he had plenty of time.

The time moved slowly as the sun began it's gradual descent towards the western horizon sending forth bright orange fingers up in the sky. At long last he saw a buggy approaching and inside sat Clyde Butcher. Jerry was very calm and deliberate as he took aim and pulled the trigger.

*   *   *   *

Eddie arrived in town at about four in the afternoon and reined up at Sam's Restaurant. He could see Larry sitting on a wooden barrel in front of Hank's Grocery and Hardware store watching the street. Everything was as it should be. Satisfied, he went on into the restaurant and took one of the tables by the front window.

"Eddie, what a nice surprise to see you so early in the day," gushed Betty as he came in.

As she moved in his direction he cut her off, "Just coffee Betty and don't bother me right now. Just let me be alone for a while. I need to think."

"You got it Sugar," was her pointed reply. Betty had learned that Eddie demanded her submission and she quickly went to the back of the restaurant after bringing Eddie his coffee.

Before long Larry came in and went over to Eddie's table. As he sat down at the table he could see Betty coming back into the room. Looking up at her he said, "Just coffee."

Both men sat at the table and waited until Betty brought the coffee over, and after topping off Eddie's cup as well she quickly went into the back room again. Only then did Larry began his report, "He's here. Got into town 'bout an hour ago and went straight into the saloon. Hasn't gone anywhere else near as I can tell."

"That's good. Now go back out and casually walk through the saloon and out the back door and come back here. I want to know if he is with someone and jus' where he is sittin' in the place." Eddie had it almost worked out but as usual he was very careful and cautious.

Ten minutes later Larry returned. "He's all alone and sittin' in the corner to the right, jus' as you walk in the door. Doing nothin' but sittin' there drinkin' a beer and waitin'."

"Great, jus' great," Eddie said excitedly. "Go back and set in front of Hank's like you were. I'll take it from here."

"It couldn't be better," he thought to himself as he looked out the window to note the position of the afternoon sun. "So Jed thought he could catch me unaware. No, he could never get the best of me." He planned to make Jed draw first in front of witnesses and he would cut him down. They would meet on his terms, and who could blame him for shooting down the man who had killed his brother in cold blood!

*   *   *   *

Jed sat patiently at the table awaiting Eddie's expected arrival. Just the sitting and waiting tended to make him drowsy after the long night fighting the fire. Perhaps he should have waited for another day. No, he could not have waited. The ranchers' meeting was set for the next morning.

The time passed slowly as a few afternoon customers came into the bar had a couple of beers and left. One who passed through was the sidekick of Eli. What was his name? Larry? Yes, Larry was the name, he remembered. He deliberated some more. I saw him at the meadow and later in here sittin' with Eddie's bunch. Strange, he just came in the front door and went out the back. Didn't even order a beer. He pondered that for a while as he continued to wait. He was sleepy and tired. Rest would have to wait as there was no turning back.

"Jed.., Jed Garrett! Come out here, you yellow coward!" was the shout from outside the building.

He recognized the voice. He rose and looked out the window. Eddie was standing across the street! "God damn it! He's changed the plans!" he exploded, but he had no choice as he moved to go out front and confront Eddie. He stepped cautiously between the swinging doors tense and ready to draw.

Eddie screamed, "There's the yellow bastard! He beat my brother to death, then shot him!"

Some shoppers on the wooden walkways stopped in frozen silence as they heard the accusation and it's implied threat, then hurriedly looked for cover.

Jed squinted into the sun as he looked across the dirt thoroughfare to see Eddie. He could hear a table being moved and people rustling about in the saloon behind him as he moved carefully to his right into the dirt road. "Damn him! He's got the sun to his advantage! I can hardly see him."

"Look at him! All nice and proper now after beating my brother to death!" Eddie continued to shout so all could hear. "There's no one to help you now you bastard! You can't run anymore! I won't let you get away after killing my brother!" he raved like a man possessed, but he knew exactly what he was doing and saying. Eddie remembered that Jed bent down slightly when he drew making a shorter target and he calculated that he had now attracted enough witnesses.

He dropped his right shoulder and jerked his arm slightly. The feint worked! Jed was drawing. Now Eddie drew faster and shot at.., the man with the rifle coming out of the saloon. It was an instinct gut reaction; a distraction attracting the first shot. Then he aimed where Jed was standing and fired again but Jed had thrown himself face down in the road to present a smaller target and that he might see to get a better shot at Eddie.

Jed fired and the bullet tore through Eddie's vest directly into his heart. There was only the stunned look of shock on Eddie's face as he twisted and fell sideways to the ground. Jed lay on his stomach in the dirt with both hands on his Colt ready to fire again if Eddie should move. There was no movement, only blood coming from Eddie's mouth. Seeing it was over Jed dropped his face in the dirt and lay unmoving and unnerved, realizing that Eddie had fired twice before he had been able to get off one shot.

People started to rush about and Jed slowly sat up in the street. Taking his time he looked around to see what Eddie had first shot at. It was Jerry Bates! Jerry had come out of the saloon as Eddie was drawing his weapon and attracted that first shot.

Jerry sat against the wall bleeding heavily from his stomach while the bartender and one of the cowboys were trying to staunch the flow of blood with some dingy bar towels. Jed moved quickly to his friend's side and knelt down. Jerry reached out to him and said weakly, "I come to tell ya'.., I shot Butcher.., he's dead!"

Doc Winters and 'Big' Ed moved through the crowd that had gathered. With the help of two of the other men standing in the crowd, the four men quickly picked Jerry up. Doc Winters shook his head sadly at Jed as they left for his office.

Jed remained by the saloon doors dazed and exhausted by everything that had happened. Eventually he got up and went inside where he sat down to gather himself and think. Nothing could be worse! Since I've been here, three men dead, four counting Butcher, and another dying.

He did not know how Jerry killed Butcher, where or why, it simply did not matter. He was dead. "I've become a killer. The town, my home, my folks, even Juanita won't be able to live with this. There will always be someone to point a finger at me."

Only later when Hank Nelson and Doc Winters rode out to the the Bates ranch to deliver the news of Jerry's death did they find John Bates dead in his chair of apparent heart failure, and after some more searching found the recently made grave of Molly Bates on the hillside. After questioning Jed, they began to realize that Jerry had indeed ambushed Clyde Butcher. The town could never figure out a reason for this and the only motive they could figure out was that perhaps Clyde had attacked and killed Molly Bates. The exact awful truth was buried and would never be known.

In the days that followed the people of Wedgewood gradually learned the complete story behind the shootings. Jed had been correct in his deductions about the the Butcher crew shooting and wounding him when the actual target was supposed to be his father. The cook for Butcher's spread acknowledged that rustling had been going on for a long time by Butcher's hired hands. It was verified too that Clyde had earlier attacked one of the Gomez girls and then set fire to the ranch to cover up the assault before running the Gomez family out of the country. The loss of the Garrett's barn by the fire was rightly attributed to Joe Swanks, and of course, to Clyde Butcher as well.

As the remaining hands at the Butcher ranch left for other areas more of Clyde's deeds became known. He had been filing on property that rightly belonged to others and then with the title in hand had run the original owners off and usurped their lands. If he couldn't get a clear title he had simply stole their livestock in larger numbers or proceeded to harass the owners until they sold out to him at prices far below the rightful values.

Even though the truth was coming out Jed had made up his mind. For the town to forget and for the wounds to heal it was time to go. His parents would forever suffer and that he could not change, but James would not have to fight the anguish and embarrassment of having a gunslinger living at home. Further he didn't want his young impressionable brother to follow his own bad example.

Still he had to set the record right by Juanita and decided to ride over to the Martinez ranch. Catching her alone they went for a short walk under the shade of the large leafy cottonwood trees by the stream behind the house.

Hesitantly Jed began, "I, ah. I'm going to leave Wedgewood for a while."

Juanita began a wry smile and a little laugh came from her mouth much to his surprise. She answered his surprised look grinning, "Jed I always knew you were leaving even if you didn't. Maybe that's the reason I love you. You aren't like other men in Wedgewood and you have this need to stand your ground. Most men try to act that way but they aren't really ready to face the consequences. Maybe the war did this to you, I really don't know. I only know you have this restfulness and you need to run free. I understand that you have to get it out of your system and if you do, come back and I'll be waiting. I'm glad we had our time together and I don't regret a bit of it."

Only now did Jed fully realize how deeply he loved her. She was obviously wise far beyond her young years. Unspeaking he took her in his arms and with tears in his eyes gave her a long loving kiss. Humbled with his head down in acknowledgment of her statement they quietly walked back to the ranch house.

The journey to seek his future could now go forth.

0-595-31536-4

Printed in the United States
19031LVS00005B/591